WHEN THE LIGHT FELL IN LOVE WITH THE FIRE

Christos Lambroudis

WHEN THE LIGHT FELL IN LOVE WITH THE FIRE

translated by
DR. DIMITRIS THANASOULAS

Pharos Books

ISBN: 978-93-55463-55-5
eISBN: 978-93-55463-61-6

©Publisher

Publisher: Pharos Books (P) Ltd.
Plot No.-55, Main Mother Dairy Road
Pandav Nagar, East Delhi-110092
Phone: 011-40395855, +14049995474
WhatsApp: +91 8368220032
E-mail: sales@pharosbooks.in
Website: www.pharosbooks.in
First Edition: 2022

Printed By: Sushma Book Binding House, Okhla
Industrial Area, Phase II, New Delhi-110020

WHEN THE LIGHT FELL IN LOVE WITH THE FIRE
CHRISTOS LAMBROUDIS

As long as I live...

My dreams are a mountainside
and my wishes are a crystal spring.
Spear pointed my ideals
and my soul's a shining shield.

No matter how high that I am gazing.
Being one with the eternal scam mountains
 I am there alone and forgotten
drinking from all the Oblivion's fountains.

And while I am closed within my silence,
then I'll be searching only for You!!!
Forever the Light I'll follow on
as long as I live, it is true...

Nowadays, very few people know the story that the Light once fell in love and became one with the Fire. I am going to narrate this story to you the way others narrated it to me. Here's how it goes:

I

Today, I'm thinking of you more than any other time...

If only you knew how much I muss you!!!

You find that strange? So long in this world. Still, I haven't found you. I never met you. I wondered so many times: "Where could you be? In which world? Which place? Which time?"

Today, for the first time in years, I felt an irrepressible need to write to you. It may be the booze. I've had one too many...(and that's an understatement!)

It's called 'alcohol'. It's the potion of Oblivion used by humans when they want to banish their thoughts and make their mind forget.

No, don't be sad. Don't worry about me. I'm neither desperate nor disappointed.

Besides, I know what Despair feels like. It's a cheap courtesan that frequents seedy places, like the one I'm in right now. I've met her in such places again and again. She gives away a few minutes of pleasure. What she wants in return is for you to give up your hope and dreams, every beautiful thought in your mind.

You're laughing, eh? That wasn't meant to be a joke. I've seen so many people pay this price without hesitation. After our first encounter, though, she didn't disturb me. I guess she realised that I'm not one for giving in to her charm.

I'm alright. Actually, I'm feeling great! So great that I'm beginning to worry. My mind right now is travelling along some weird paths...

I don't mind the hazy atmosphere in here with the smoke. Even the icy-cold expressionless look the cards lying on the floor are giving me seems so familiar.

These cards are used by charlatans, who toy with people's dreams and expectations of the future...

You know, that's what people are like in this world: icy-cold and expressionless!

They let their emotions wear off. They put a mask on their instincts and passions to make them look like emotions. This way, they think they fill the void within. You should see how they cringe away when they come across a real emotion...

They're scared!!! They're afraid to give and take emotions!!! Unfortunately, I took a long time to realise that. I unwittingly hurt people every time I tried to share my feelings.

There's something I need to confess to you. Don't hold a grudge against me, though. Yes, I've mated with some of them in the past. In the end, absence is stronger than presence.

At times when your absence was so strong, I mistook them for you. I thought they were you. Maybe I wished they were you. My strong desire to meet you was to blame...

Forgive me. When you sorely miss someone, you see their face and hear their voice wherever you go.

I'd rather be on my own. I no longer wish to create or obtain anything. Why should I, after all? You're not here. When you can't share anything with someone, it's like you don't even have it.

I ended up standing on top of my loneliness. I'm looking around from above. I'm a wandering shadow in the eyes of those who see me from below.

"So what?" you say. "Everyone's alone, after all, right?"

No, it's not the same. My loneliness is completely different.

"Does it matter?" you ask.

Yes, it does to me...

People here are lovely because they shielded themselves. They try to hide their weaknesses, their phobias, themselves. They don't accept anything as is. They treat everything on the basis of how they would like things to be. That's why they become hostile towards what differs from them.

Many times, I've seen them cut up rough and become so hostile and fierce without any logical explanation. With time, I came to realise that they're simply scared. They violently try to mask their weaknesses and phobias...

I want you to know, though, that I never tried to hide. I've never felt disgusted at my own reflection in the mirror.

I always try to keep my soul alive. However, this world has turned into an infectious disease. On many occasions, I felt like I was infected myself.

Each time, though, I miraculously got over it. This may be a gift I brought from my own world, the place where I come from. Where do I come from, really?

I'm concerned about the ease with which I seem to overcome everything. Is it because a part of myself has died?

Time and again, I tried to ruin myself singlehandedly. Time and again, I hastened to take delight in the thought that I was on the brink of disaster, in a dubious state, yet I...

Nothing gets me down. Nothing can hurt me!!! There's a Dark Force that fights and haunts me. But there's also something that protects me. Something oozes out of me that heals everything!!!

On countless occasions, I've caught myself shouting indignantly:

"Isn't there anyone out there capable of dealing me a death blow?"

All this becomes yet another stone in a wall that's slowly and gradually being erected. It begins to surround me, while I'm on top of my loneliness. With the passage of time, I'm cloistering myself more and more...

I don't belong here, I know!!!

Thousands of people go past me every day. I can't sense their presence. I don't know why. I can't even understand what it is that they see in me. I guess they feel there's something different about me.

That I am something different. That I'm not a human being!!!

Like I said earlier, what is different, people try to absorb or destroy it. In my case, they haven't achieved that yet...

You see how my loneliness differs from that of other people? Everything around me seems so fragile...

What is loneliness? What is Loneliness herself?

It's so remarkable that every word makes its own journey. But people don't seem to know it. You must have the eyes of your soul open to be able to gaze at immense heights. You must be able and your gaze should pierce through unfathomable depths in order to discover this journey.

The journey of words starts from the sky and ends up a destination in people's minds. Through this course, they discover their meaning. To put it differently, what their real interpretation is.

Is the value of being alone akin to loneliness? Is whoever is suffused with loneliness alone? When someone chooses to be alone out of conviction, doesn't their loneliness carry any value?

Questions too come from the sky, while answers are unexplored routes. Which lead to unknown destinations as well...

I'm afraid to touch what I love, so as not to destroy it. I'm afraid to approach what I most desire, so that it won't go away. Maybe there's a reason that I am here in this world.

Still, I don't know what to do. Should I search for this reason? Shall I carry on searching for you? How about trying to discover the gate through which I will go back where I come from? All this seems so infeasible right now. The truth is, I'm tired...

I want to write you so much more, but I don't know where you are, I don't know where to send this letter.

They say thoughts don't go away; they simply travel forever. I hope the thoughts I'm sending you will find you. Wherever you are. To remind you that I haven't forgotten you. That I think of you all the time.

We're going to meet in another life, in another world and time!!!

Till then, cherish my thoughts, so that they will keep you company...

2

Hardly a moment passes without my wondering. Do my thoughts find you? Do they reach you? Or do they travel eternally, like the hazy light of a star on a no-return journey to the unknown?

Not even I can remember how long I've been wandering around. It all started suddenly when I opened my eyes. I realised that I was in a foreign unknown world. I'm still trying to understand if all this is real. Am I awake inside a dream?

I wander around, looking for answers. I have to find out who I am, how I ended up here. My questions, all the things I have to figure out, began to get entangled, like the links in a chain on me. I feel it weigh down on me, chocking me. What's really going on with me?

I have to find out why I'm here. How am I going to release myself? Everything around me is like a rotten cobwebbed stage, with shadows-extras aimlessly loitering, playing a dull vacuous part...

Everyone around me plays characters so different from what they really are. They play roles, feigning persons who don't tally with their real selves. They do things that are not actually theirs.

I still haven't figured out if they do it to fool themselves or what it is that haunts them. I guess they're unable to understand that it's no use hiding away.

I miss my little friend. The only being I came in contact with in this world. The only creature that kept me company for a few moments. The only entity that seemed so real to me!

One day, while I was walking, I stumbled upon a place where evening primroses had grown. You know them? They are some beautiful small purple flowers. They're called this way as they open their petals only at night. They smell fantastic!!!

This is my little friend. An evening primrose I came across one morning. I saw that one of them was open in the sunlight.

At first, I thought it was a chance event. However, every single morning I saw the same flower opening up, unlike the rest. It wasn't a coincidence...

You can't imagine what impression it made on me. It actually reminded me of myself. This small flower had renounced darkness. Every single day, it stubbornly opened its petals to the sunlight.

So, I went there to check on it every dawn. I touched it. I spoke to it. I sang to it. We had become very good friends. It was the only being I felt I could open my heart to. I've told it about you...

You should have seen how it responded. It tried to talk to me as well. I could feel it. I saw it in its moves!!!

Could it be that it knew where you were? Was it trying to find a way to tell me? How beautiful this world would be if everyone followed the example of this small primrose...

All this until one dawn I went to see my little friend once again. As I looked at its side from a distance, I saw it with its petals closed, just like the rest.

I froze!!! I shuddered at the thought that it couldn't stand its loneliness and the price it had to pay for its audacity and it gave up. Maybe an incident that had happened earlier was to blame...

Where I was, a crow flew over me. The crow is considered the Messenger of Death, a bad omen. People are afraid of Death. I know that very well. So, I menacingly reached out my hand.

"Don't worry. I didn't come here for you," it squawked in its throaty voice, then it flew out of my sight...

What is it that people fear about Death? Does Death really exist? If so, wouldn't He die as well?

When Hopes fall off the rocks of Despair, isn't this Death as well? When the Soul is locked up in the wet and dark prison in the dungeons of the Tower of Oblivion, isn't this Death as well?

Could Death simply be an End? But doesn't every single End have a new Beginning? Is it possible that there is only Life, a perennial hidden secret?

Some people say that you only live once. That means we'd better live every single moment as if it were our last one. Others say that this is wrong. You live on an everyday basis. We only die once…

What can one say about me, though? It's like I'm living an everyday repetitive death, while I'm gasping for air…

You know, they promised me a breath of life more than once. All I had to do was don a fantasy or worship a false idol. What breath of life could that be that came at such a price?

I refused!!!

I'd rather live my everyday repetitive death…

It's plain to see that people are not only afraid of what is different from them, but also what they do know. No, I won't do what other people do. I won't fall victim to their barren logic. It doesn't take only a simple choice between the Light and Darkness…

The Light is a Shine that guides. It's also a Flame ready to sear whoever is not ready for it.

Darkness disorients the traveller. Through Darkness, though, the Light looks stronger…

That's what I was thinking as I approached. I was anxious to see what had become of my little friend. I figured out what happened. I smiled from ear to ear.

My little friend had found a mate!!!

You should have been here with me. You should have seen how its petals were entangled with those of another flower. They were like two faces locked in an eternal kiss and they would never open or close their petals again.

When it was on its own, this small flower renounced the Light. Now that it had found its match, it had gone well beyond the Light. How grand and inconceivable for all us who bear the Fall!!!

It was time for us to go our separate ways. Autumn was nearing, after all. Many of the flowers had already fallen to the ground. Its turn was only a matter of time. It would then embark on a new journey in the Earth's embrace, so that it would be reborn. This time, though, it won't be alone anymore…

I had mixed feelings. On the one hand, I was elated. On the other, however, I lost a special friend. Perhaps I also missed a rare opportunity to find out if you exist…

I'll never say goodbye to you, my little friend. You never said goodbye to me either. It's not necessary, after all. Only bodies separate and keep distances. Ours is a strong bond that will never get lost!!!

When two souls forge an inviolable eternal bond, they are overcome with so many emotions that cannot be put into words.

There are times when words are not enough to put things into perspective, that's why we must not downplay the 'power of silence'.

> Tell me, have you ever heard the cry of Silence?
> Believe me, nothing is louder than its cry.
> Silence can express grandeur in its real proportions.
> You can even hear it in people's sullen looks.
> In there, countless wounded dreams and betrayed expectations
> holler at the top of their lungs: "UNTIL WHEN?"
> You can also hear it in the reflections of the mirror
> that look at you, icy-cold and silent,
> while loneliness and absence echo on the vast
> walls of your mind's dark labyrinths,
> howling "WHY?"
> Try as you might to close your ears,
> you can't escape the Silence.
> Don't you ever underestimate it
> as nothing is louder than its cry...

Silence itself has a huge power when it has a content. Silence itself can be stronger than a thousand cries. One must only be in a position to listen out for it...

Amid such a silence, which could express grandeur, we were fellow travellers on a journey where our paths crossed for a few fleeting moments. These moments were so unique and rare that I will never forget them. You can't even imagine how much I've learnt from you through your silence in such a short period of time.

I wholeheartedly hope that you found what you were looking for and your journey had the ending you desired. My duty is to carry on with my own silent ride to loneliness. Until I find my own destination too...

3

The storm won't blow over.
The rain is incessantly whipping the shutters.
The hiss of the wind sounds more threatening than ever.
Thunderbolts!!!
Everything has plunged into darkness.
There is nothing else but myself and the storm…
Sometimes, I only make out my own reflection
on the pane of glass for split seconds,
thanks to the lightning.
There is something different about this storm…
It seems to have come to me to call out my name…

Suddenly, at every burst of lightning, strange images gibe place to my reflection on the glass. Like some distant memories come alive. I can clearly see pictures. With time, it all becomes so vivid.

Hang on! That's me!!! I remember now. The scream of my rage, though, wasn't enough to deaden the sounds of the storm. That was my howl: an angry and drawn-out 'aaaaaaaahhhhh'…

I wonder. A is the first sound in human languages. It is these sounds that form the words. A is the first in the line, even of the symbols humans use to turn speech into writing. The first symbol is a.

Isn't A, in all its forms, a start? There's an 'a' in 'start'…

The strangest thing of all is that, while 'a' represent a start, people put it at the beginning (or close to the beginning) of many words, in order to denote absence, lack and deprivation. This 'a' may take the form of 'un', 'in' or 'dis' in various languages.

When, for example, they say unawareness, they mean lack of knowledge. When they speak of inanity, they mean lack of understanding. When someone is inexperienced, this means they lack experience. A start that is put at the beginning of a word means absence, which starts with an 'a' as well. I'd like to know how many such 'a's' came out with my howl...

Am I a fallen angel? If so, this explains everything.

I'm trying to understand. I wonder if I unwittingly fooled around with Hubris or if you were my own Hubris. What envious fate hurled me among the Sirens and the Furies?

I decided to leave everything behind me. Dressed in tatters, I ended up crossing the desert.

On my back hang what used to be my wings, two repugnant masses. I still carry my rusty weapons as a reminder of my former grandeur.

And I move on...

Someone who once lay in the Light and is now moving among the Shadows. They closed the doors to me, even in the most hospitable places. Even the most well-meaning people turned me away. When they see me, their faces change straight away. I can clearly see their envy and aversion.

They don't give a toss about my comedown. No one asks who stuck this spear into my back. They take no heed of my wound, which is gradually growing and making my flesh rot.

They chafe at my former wings!!! No matter what happens, however deep I fall, this will never change. They will be jealous of my former wings...

They take me for a lunatic...When a limb is amputated, you still feel it's there. Maybe till they die.

Just like me: even if nothing is visible on me, I still feel these wings on my back. As for the pang of the spear, there may still be a wound there. Many a time, I can feel the pain, which is unbearable...

You wonder? You puzzle? You're incredulous? You ask why all these people have gathered around me? Why they are arguing? How can you be so naive?

They gathered around me out of curiosity. To see what looks like a 'transformed eyesore' to them. Can't you hear their voices? 'The Fallen One is here. Come and see the Lapsi!!!'

You really believe they're arguing over who's going to lay claim to you or to something I have? You know full well that I don't have anything anyone would desire...

They're arguing over who will be ceded pride of place, so that they'll take a closer look at me. Why do you think they're reaching out their hand to me? To help me up, so that I won't stumble?

Look at their smile. They're looking at me, satisfying their vanity, the Hymns to their arrogance. They cannot understand that it's their own Requiem...

I've just realised why the little primrose kept silent and wouldn't speak to me. He wanted to stop me from remembering...

Don't worry. Nothing can get me down anymore. No chain is able to hold me back from being away from you, no world, no time.

I will rise again — I can vouch for that!

Until then, simply cherish my thoughts...

4

Desert...
The personification of the harmony of Chaos.
Vastness!!!
Where nothing is what it seems...
The place where, once you wake up, nothing is the same...
The ark where primeval memories are kept.
Where perennial opposites clash but co-exist.
Where death traps lurk every inch of the way
for those who are not privy to its secrets...
Where illusions and mirages
stroke your ears like whispers,
expecting to lure you into
the Land of Oblivion!!!
Where the day is the ordeal of the fiery inferno!!!
While at night...
Tell me, have you ever spent the night in the desert?
When the song of the icy-cold wind meets the loneliness
of the traveller in the frozen darkness?
When everything looks like the void of the soul when it is betrayed
by the tears of sorrow?
Like a voracious Abyss that lies in ambush for every Lost Soul,
so as to feed on his futile arrogance?
Not even I can remember when I chose to cross the desert
at night...

Why do I avoid residential areas? I'm tired of mobs point their finger at me. Of their gathering around me. Of their turning their back on when their curiosity has been satisfied.

I'm tired of seeing them smile nastily, feeling happy not to be in my place, while in fact they're ostensibly safe in their ignorance.

At least in the desert at night, you know you're walking alone, accompanied by the wind's song in the frozen dark, guided by the blue moonlight.

The Moon, which the ignoramuses curse as the daughter of 'Evil'. They do not know that it's her own light that guides, so that no one gets lost when walking along dark paths...

Yet another night walk in the desert...

Once the day is over, the sun is gone, taking along its fiery breaths. Until I rise, I have to know how to co-exist with the Shadows...

Then, the wind appears to soothe the traveller. Just like serenity in the mind of a madman, who is lost in his dad and otherworldly thoughts, gradually transforming like the frozen void of a soul that has just seen its dreams and goals tumble down...

Why do you find my words strange? But another strange thing happened tonight...

While I was travelling, following once again the hiss of the wind, I heard some chirps. I listened out for a moment to make sure this wasn't a figment of my imagination. Then, my heart, slave to her obsession over you, shivered!!!

I thought it was your call. For a moment, I forgot about every wound over my body. I felt every nightmare that haunted me was gone. I quickened my gait and followed this call until I reached a place with lush vegetation.

How weird...How could there be such a place in the heart of the desert? I went closer. I thought I heard voices. Suddenly, these voices ceased.

"Who's there?" I asked. I got no reply.

All I could hear was the babble of a source. After a while, I heard whispers, which had a strange childlike timbre. But this sounded so otherworldly to me.

I couldn't make out what they were saying. The last thing I heard was a phrase: "How can this be possible?" What I managed to understand was their puzzlement over the fact that I could hear them.

I asked once again: "Who's there?" Then, some hazy figures turned up in front of me.

I heard one of them say: "Of course! It's Aiaibamon!!!"

I found myself in the place where the spirits of the desert gather at nights. That's where they get together and narrate what they encountered during the day.

Is that how I'm known among the world of spirits? Is this my real name? Aiaibamon? The one who wanders around?

The spirits welcomed me cordially. It was the first time in my life that I had felt so welcome. I joined them. I listened to their stories. I spoke and had a laugh with them. We said some things I'd better tell you when we get together...

At some point, though, I couldn't take it any longer. I asked them about you. I asked them if you exist. If you do exist, do they know where you are?

"Questions come from the sky. Answers are unknown courses towards explored destinations" was their answer.

I stared at them, waiting for something more. Then, they told me that, even if they wanted to, even if they knew, they couldn't reveal such a thing. It's something I have to discover by myself.

I was overcome with sorrow...

The spirits, then, wanted to reassure me. They consoled me. They asked me to look inside the waters of the spring. I carried out their order without a second thought.

In the waters of the spring that reflected the blue moonlight I saw a bright winged form. Behind this figure, I saw images of an unknown, yet so familiar, place. I also saw three suns and seven moons.

I was puzzled...

"Who's that? What's this place?" I asked the spirits.

"This is your real form," said the spirits. "You are between two worlds. That's the reason why you can hear and see us, no matter how hazily. That's something humans can't do. You're seen differently in the world of humans and the world of spirits."

"So, who am I? What am I? What's going on with me?" I shouted.

"If you keep contacting both worlds, you have nothing to fear" were their last words. Then, they disappeared. Once again, I was left alone, feeling I'd lost yet another bond with the world of humans...

I had to carry on. Dawn would break in a while. I didn't have the time to go very far away. I thought I heard a child crying. A few yards away was seated a little girl. She was sobbing.

I thought I had to help her. I wasn't sure if she would see me with the eyes of her childish soul or those of a human. I went closer, my face covered. I didn't want her to see it. I didn't want her to realise what I was…

"What's the matter?" I asked her.

"I got lost," she replied in a quivering voice.

I reassured her by holding her in my arms. I then carried on.

The girl uncovered my face. She put her hand on my cheek. She smiled at me. I felt a warm stroke in my soul. Two wet paths mingled under my eyes.

I gave her a tight hug!

It was dawning. The sky doffed the mantle of the night. It was surrounded with the 'Twilight of Gods'.

I could make out some rooftops on the horizon.

"Is that where your home is?" I asked her. She nodded.

We went closer. I didn't want to go any near that residential area. I put her down, so that she could go back to her family.

She didn't go very far. At some point, she stopped short and came back to me. She raised her hand, her finger pointing to the sky. I looked far afield, beyond the clouds, only to see countless flocks of migratory birds.

"Do you know that these birds travel far and wide, covering huge distances?" she asked.

I nodded my head.

"That's what our thoughts are like. They set off on a journey to the unknown. Every so often, though, they rest in some people's hearts, staining them with the colour of their wings. So, don't worry. Your course is not in vain."

I looked at her in puzzlement…

She smiled at me. She ran away towards the village, where she vanished out of sight…

5

I often believed that magic is gone from this world. But something always happened to give me the lie...

Tell me, have you ever seen fireflies dance?

Fireflies are some winged creatures. They glow in the dark. When they start dancing, they look like stardust drenched in light that sneaked out of a divine hand before it fell on Earth. So beautiful is their dance!!!

I still remember the first time I saw them. What a pity once again! You're not here with me in this world, so you can't see them...

This world keeps confusing me. It holds surprises all the time, either pleasant or unpleasant. Almost everything is unknown to me. Many a time, I feel my eyes are like those of a newborn baby whose every single glance is a new discovery.

You will surely ask me: "After so long, haven't you discovered what you're looking for? Haven't you realised who you are? Haven't you found the path that will lead you to your destination?"

The answer is: "No!!!" But I know what I'm looking for. I also discovered who I am NOT. Which roads not to take. That's better than nothing. Let's not weary you with all these thoughts...

It was nighttime. I came across a small river. I decided to follow its course. Maybe because I remembered the spirits I had crossed paths with. They told me that creatures of other words hand around in sources and rivers...

I was hoping that maybe I would meet some of them again to get the answers I sought. I was going down the road, alongside this small river, when I heard a tune coming from afar.

I once again believed it was the Wind that used to sing at nights. When I went closer, though, I realised it was a melody coming from a string instrument.

In a clearing, I saw a fire and a young boy seated under a tree. I don't know why, but I decided to go closer. Perhaps I did that out of curiosity or because I hadn't spoken to someone in a long time. But I don't think this is important...

A neigh was heard. The horse accompanying the young boy sensed my presence.

The boy looked at me, unruffled. As I approach him, he smilingly said:

"Welcome, stranger. My name is Shira-Tuth. Come. Sit by the fire to get some rest."

He welcomed me cordially. He probably didn't understand what I was. Probably because darkness hid so much about me, projecting my fuzzy figure through the flickering light of the fire. But his horse didn't react either.

Animals sense lots of things of which humans don't have the slightest idea. I felt relieved. I smiled back.

"Do you have a name your folks call you by?" he asked.

"Aiai...er...," I hesitated for a few seconds. "You can call me Pyr-Kaa," I said.

I don't know how on earth I made up that name. I thought it'd be best not to speak and reveal anything about my conversation with the spirits.

"So, you are the flame that came from nowhere..." (that's what it means in humans' language), he said smilingly. "You have a strange name, stranger. Join us. You're welcome."

I asked him how he had got there and what he was doing all alone in that place. He then started narrating his story.

He spoke of the joy and pride he felt. A few days earlier, he had passed the 'manhood ceremony' with flying colours. It was an ancient custom of his people whose origins dated far back into the mists of time...

He explained to me that this ceremony was one of the most significant events for every young man in Len-Bion. That was the place where he came from and which was far away.

It was an event that took place when it was time for someone to come of age. It marked their lives forever. Passing this ceremony with success played an important role in their social existence.

Every man who turned fifteen must win the right to be considered a man on his own merit. One of the things he would earn was the name by which he would be called.

To achieve this, he had to pass the following procedure: he would hunt and kill or trap a forest animal on his own.

The deadline was from the sun rise of the 'Day of the Sun' to the next sunset. Every year, children and adults in Len-Bion waited for this 'Day of the Sun' with bated breath.

That was the day when the sun lasted the longest. It was then that the 'manhood ceremony' took place. That day was a feast.

Unless you passed this ceremony with success, you couldn't have a family or participate in the community. You couldn't be considered a warrior and, above all, you couldn't have a name!

As he explained later on, people in Len-Bion regarded name as something sacred. It was what gave the soul existence. Every new existence was unique. When someone knew someone's real name, they could captivate their soul through magic.

They also believed that gods knew everything in this world thanks to their real names. That's why only your parents knew your real name. They also thought that even animals and birds had names.

"Fortunately, humans don't know their language anymore. It would be scary for someone to trap their soul...," I thought.

When it was Shira-Tuth's turn to go through this ceremony (that was the name he had earned), he didn't have to go very far in order to find an opponent. As soon as he took a few steps towards the forest, he heard a strange sound coming from the sky.

He raised his head and saw an eagle charge a baby left lying under a tree. The baby's parents were watching the ceremony. They couldn't even imagine what risk their child was running at the time.

Within split seconds, he took out his bow. He took aim with an instinctive move. Slightly afterwards, the eagle was falling to the ground, pierced by his arrow.

He couldn't keep his broad smile in check, replete with joy and satisfaction, when he described how the crowd broke into applause.

The baby's parents realised what happened. They couldn't stop thanking him, teary-eyed. They were so happy that they gifted him this wonderful red hose with a golden mane. He called it 'Gror', which means 'thunder'.

Luckily, these people were horse breeders. That's why their choice of gift was so generous. From the word go, it was evident that they took to one another. This proud steed was his loyal companion.

He also told me that the committee of the ceremony comprising some old men was impressed by this fact. He didn't only calculate the distance and speed of the wind, but also that of the eagle.

No one else in the history of Len-Bion had ever successfully passed this test so quickly. This was quite an honour for him.

The old men considered him successful. They called him 'Shira-Tuth', which meant 'the one who looks high'. Until then, he had been known as simply 'Iman's son, the blacksmith's child.

He proudly showed me his bow. It was his father's gift. He had carved it for him out of oakwood.

He had been carving it for months, so that it would be hard and weighed. It took him a long time to make the chord, which was from a tiger's intestine. Still, he had to make sure it was as strong and elastic as possible.

It took him even longer to make the pretty engraved handle. He also took pains to carve the arrows, adding metal heads to them.

"Nothing could ever describe Iman's joy and pride regarding his son when he saw the result," I said to myself.

Shira-Tuth was so trilled that he roamed the forests and wilderness. He meant to become Len-Bion's best archer!!!

I can't deny that this little boy's smile was contagious, no matter how marginally.

I liked hearing him speak of his juvenile achievements, his youthful dreams. He was so energetic and passionate about life as he spoke!!!

Dreams are like ships
preparing for a long voyage.
People have them when they are young
and these stand at the ready,
brand new and polished at their port,
awaiting the kick-off signal.
But the way is full of storms, tempests, stillness...
It's also fraught with reefs and rocks!!!
Very few of them will reach their destination,
maybe none!!!

Most people know that,
yet they are not discouraged from supplying them
and sending them into the open Ocean of their life.

Aren't people strange? I still can't explain their behaviour when it comes to certain things...

When the boy completed his narration, he asked me how someone earned their name in my place.

My place...

I could hardly stifle a spontaneous sarcastic laugh. How would I know — who would tell me — what my place was like?

I wanted to give an answer that would satisfy him. He deserved it, after lal. Fortunately, I didn't have to think very hard.

"In my place, each one's actions determine their name," I told him.

The boy cracked a smile and nodded his head.

At some point, our conversation drew to a close. For a few moments, we stayed silent. Then, I saw his string instrument. It was placed on the grass by his side. As he said, it was named Kira. It was made from carved wood.

Shira-Tuth understood. He handed it to me.

"Play," he urged me.

I politely refused. I explained that I didn't know how to play an instrument. Still, I asked him to play if he was partial to a melody. He seemed to hesitate for a moment. Suddenly, though, he had a mysterious inspiration.

He grabbed hold of the Kira and started playing a weird plaintive tune, while singing:

"I saw you reaching out to the sky,
begging the sun and I puzzled.
On your snow-white veil
Iris was playing some unprecedented games and I wept.
In your shiny hair
hid stars
that wanted to escape the veil of the night
to keep you company
and I wept."

Amid that melancholic tone, which was coupled with a soft sweet sense, nature around us fell silent for a few moments. She too wanted to listen to Shira-Tuth's song.

Not even the nightbirds were heard. Only the small river flowing next to us carried on gurgling, as if accompanying that melody.

Gradually, every living being around the area joined in. They all wanted to partake of those harmonious sounds that spread through the night. The birds, the crickets, the rustling leaves of the trees — everything completed this song.

It was then that I saw it!!! I saw the dance of the fireflies a few metres away from the fire. Hundreds of them flying frenziedly, like stardust falling from the sky!!!

Theirs was a light dance, like they were trying to tell me:

"Don't worry, don't give up on your journey. Your soul is strong. Trust it and you'll make it."

I watched them, speechless. I couldn't believe what I saw. How many wondrous things could this world hide?

At some point, the melody ceased. Along with it ceased the fireflies, like shooting stars that scatter their leftovers all around...

6

His gaze was fixed on the ground. I caught myself being lost in thought. After a while, out of the corner of my eye, I saw Shira-Tuth give me a strange look. He couldn't tear his eyes from me.

It was plain to see. He was surprised at my reaction. I could tell he wanted to speak, but he hesitated. At some point, he plucked up the courage to open his mouth.

"Is there someone you think of all the time, Pyr-Kaa?" he asked me.

I nodded my head.

"And you feel pain every time you think of her image?"

"That's right," I replied in a low voice, my eyes fixed on him.

"There are some things I cannot understand, Pyr-Kaa," Shira-Tuth continued. "Why do all those who speak of love do so in the same way? Why is something that should be beautiful expressed with so much pain?"

I forced a smile.

There are some people who believe that it's much easier to confide something that is troubling you to a complete stranger.

The fact that they don't know you makes their judgement objective. The knowledge that you're unlikely to see them again makes you feel free and secure.

That's what I resolved to do. Not to reveal to him who I was. I would talk to him about you. He seemed to take a genuine interest.

There are times when words are unnecessary. They are unable to describe events or put emotions in the right perspective. Still, sometimes words can prove stronger than actions themselves.

When words find their destination, they reveal their real power. Like a spark of consolation, sympathy and inspiration, they can flare up and become a flame, spreading all over the place, goading a soul into acts of grandeur!!!

So, I began to talk to the boy about your calling that overwhelms me. About all my feelings and how desperately I seek you.

The pain caused by the image of you inside of me,
which is not exactly pain.
That feeling of constriction in the heart and all over the body.
The power I feel inside of me when I think of you,
but I cannot understand where it comes from.
How strong and insignificant I feel,
capable of everything,
but at the same time completely impotent.

I also told him that I don't even know if you exist. But, even if you do exist, maybe you don't know about my existence. You may not have an inkling...

I got upset; you could tell from my tone of voice!!!

I realised as I spoke that Shira-Tuth couldn't stand seeing me in this state. He wanted to do something — it was obvious. He didn't know what, though.

He sat next to me. I made to react. I don't want people to touch me!!! Every time someone touched me, their touch relayed all their countless negative emotions. I felt their pain, their phobias, their greed, even their envy and all evil.

It's so painful and distressing feeling people's inner world. I avoid it at all costs. That little girl was the only exception. I didn't feel anything negative about him either. I remained unflappable.

"Pyr-Kaa, I really don't know what to say," he said. "What you say is very weird. I don't know what to say or do. I wish I could help you. I'll only say one thing: I don't know why, but I envy you! What you feel may give you the impression that it causes you hurt. Still, to me it seems unique and important!!! I can't hide that, after all I've heard, I'd like to be in this state, without any regard for what will come next. Let's not fool ourselves, my friend. What's life worth without emotions? What's an icy-cold life shorn of emotions and interest in aid of? All these are emotions, my friend. We have to feel them, no matter what they are and where they come from. We simply have to feel them. It's this alternation of theirs that gives meaning to life. Through realising others' value. That's why you should count yourself lucky. Yes, you're lucky, since you can feel something as unique as that. As for her, it doesn't matter whether she knows it or she'll ever find out. Not even what she feels. What counts is what YOU feel!!! You never know: maybe all this is the gods' will. You can never tell what they want to do or what their plans are. Don't be like that, my friend. Try to look at things from a different point of view."

I hesitantly smiled.

"The Gods not only can't help me, but I doubt whether they even care about me...," I thought.

Still, I rejoiced in his words, which I found so comforting. I raised my eyes and thanked him. He really made me feel better.

Shira-Tuth was happy that his words had had an impact on me.

"You know, Pyr-Kaa," he told me, "I believe that every human being is made for a specific person."

"The poor boy doesn't know that I am not human...," a cynical thought crossed my mind.

"When you find this man," he continued, "you feel complete. All burdens and sorrow are cut in two when you share them, whereas joy is doubled. There is a story in my place, according to which humans used to be neither male nor female, but something in between. At some point, gods, for their own reasons, cut them in two. That's how men and women were created. Since then, every piece has been looking for its other half. Don't thank me. Like I said earlier, I wish I could do something. I wholeheartedly hope that you'll find what you're looking for."

"You've done much more than you think," I thought as I smiled upon hearing his words.

I must admit that I liked that story he narrated. That humans were split in two and now each piece is looking for its other half.

But it was time to go to sleep. We lay by the fire. If only its flame could warm the cockles of my heart and my flesh.

There is hope, after all, that people may change. This hope is embodied by that boy. Maybe I shouldn't treat all people the same way. With the right guidance, maybe humans as a species will evolve into something better.

While I was mulling all this over, I started to feel my body growing heavy. Sleep was gradually seizing it...

7

Is there a dividing line between reality and fantasy in the realm of humans? What is imagination and what are dreams? Are they related?

People don't dream only in their everyday life. They dream when they sleep as well. Are dreams simple images carved out of hidden desires?

Are they the substance that urges us to blaze a trail we aspire with the passage of time? Every single dream could be a godsend. Like a guide that comes to carve a path.

Could imagination be a flask drenched in dreams that could serve as a rejuvenating infusion that allays human pain inflicted by life's hardships, or as an opium for the weak and desperate seeking a way out of illusion?

I've always felt I didn't need dreams. I neither remember them nor have any in my sleep.

Maybe people need them as they have limited potential. This is the only way they have to pave the way for the Land of Imagination. In any other case, this might never happen...

But I'm not human...

I may believe this simply because I tried to fool or console myself. For something I thought I don't have and may never acquire — dreams!!!

Then, one night, I had a nightmare...

It was the first time I had ever had a dream in this world. It seems that, whatever that might be, it decided to carry on even in my dreams.

I saw I was a bright sun. One starry night, I met a small distant star across the vastness of the sky. I sent it a stroke with my ray. It smiled at me. Then, I was gripped by an irrepressible desire to travel and meet that small star.

I became one with my ray of light. I decided to follow it in order to reach that star. Along with it, I wanted to touch infinity. So, I set off on my voyage to the ends of the universe...

When I approached it, the small star drew back in fear. I realised it was being seared by me. I never thought my rays would ever harm it. I could never imagine my light would hurt it.

How can the sunlight hurt? Still, it was a small star used to shining in a dark sky. Light scares those who are not used to it. Why hadn't it ever occurred to me?

It's my fault. Would it believe me if I explained to it? I should have known it would dread my explosions.

If I could ask Time for a wish,
that would be to get me back.
At the right time, so that I would hide my rays.
Now it will never believe me!
The very fire of mine burnt everything.
Everything was gone...
Like tomorrow's expectations
that are dashed today...

I'll have no other chance. Now it will remain a wounded star shining in a dark sky. I must leave, under the weight of responsibility. I wish I could make amends.

If I could ask Time for a wish,
that would be to get me back.
The time I was travelling to it.
My light would embrace it.
It wouldn't be left alone in a dark sky.
If only I could give it Eternity.

I let out a cry of indignation: "I refuse to be the Sun!!! Let my rays spread into every single corner of the universe. I don't deserve them, nor do I want them!!!

Let me be a comet doomed to travel on its own. A cold amorphous body caught up in the same dull solitary circle, while groping in the icy-cold dark...

Then, I transformed into a star to visit Earth. I travelled to the distant ends of the universe. I became a bright star to offer beauty to the desolate dark sky.

Those who saw me at first marvelled at me, smiled and made a wish. In the end, though, that's the only thing I remained for everyone — simply a wish...

They all wanted me as a wish. When I became a shooting star in order to grant all these wishes, no one reached out their hand to pick up my stardust. I disappeared when my shine wore off in the silence of the night...

I woke up in fright. I broke out in a cold sweat. Thousands of questions flashed through my mind.

At some point, I felt like screaming, calling out your name. Still, no sound came out of my mouth. Ignoring your name slit my throat like a blade. I wondered once again if you exist.

I opened my eyes, but the only thing I saw was darkness!!!

Vast thick darkness...

8

If you exist, do you want to see me?

In order for a human to see me, they must take off their masks. After all, human eyes cannot see what is really there. A mask, no matter how well it covers, stops them even more from seeing what they want to hide and are already unable to see before them.

If they take off their masks, if they close their human eyes and open those of their souls, they may be able to see my figure against a real backdrop. From now on, I refuse to exist inside anything phoney...

How would you see me?

If you exist, do you want to find me?

In order for a human to find me, they must look for autumn under the trees. They would find me if they made it through the fallen leaves. That's where I'm waiting to become one with the ground.

That's where I'll be ready to get reborn in a new Spring. From now on, I refuse to be part of a dead dry branch, at the mercy of the winter...

How would you try to find me?

If you exist, do you want to hear me?

In order for a human to hear me, they must first listen out for the Night's sounds. Only then will they be able to hear my voice.

I'll hide in the stars that flicker as they play. I'll be among the setting sun rays. From now on, I refuse to see the works of darkness in broad daylight...

How would you try to hear my voice?

Are you the stuff dreams, wishes and desires are made on?

"You dream out loud and think even louder," a voice interrupted my thoughts.

I jumped up in fright. I was struck by the fact that what I heard wasn't like a sound but rather a voice inside my head.

At first, I thought it was the boy. But as I turned around, I saw him sleeping by the fire.

I looked around. All I could see was the fog that glistened in the twilight. I stood up and walked a few yards away. Suddenly, through the veil of the fog, a form hove into view. At first, I thought I saw a horse. My first thought was that a rider myst be there somewhere.

"Who is it?" I asked in a loud voice.

"I'm Leukarat," she said, "your new friend."

I realised there was no rider. The horse was talking to me. I let out a cross between a laugh and an exclamation of awkwardness. I must confess I was taken aback.

"Leukarat, in magic creatures' language, means White Beauty," the voice continued.

"What are you?" I asked.

"I'm a female unicorn," she replied.

I'd heard of these creatures, but I couldn't tell whether they really existed.

Unicorns look like horses. In fact, they're magic creatures. You can recognise them by the carved horn on their forehead and the shine that envelops them.

"How did you find me, White Beauty?" I asked.

My interest was growing. After a while, I saw a snow-white winged Unicorn before me.

They say that winged unicorns are a rare species. I watched this snow-white unicorn with admiration, until I heard her voice inside my head again:

"Like I said, you dream out loud and think even louder," she answered. "I was nearby. I heard your dreams and thoughts. Although I didn't mean to, I overheard everything. I found out that you're not human. Now I know you need answers and some help..."

Her words piqued my curiosity.

We talked for a while. I discovered that it was a wonderful being. She had a knack for hearing everyone's thoughts. Instead of speaking, she conveyed her thoughts to others. They sounded like a voice inside my head. That's how she communicated.

She told me about her species, the magic creatures, their habits and the reasons why they avoided humans, choosing these specific hours to roam the world.

She had one more reason to avoid humans. As she could hear thoughts, it didn't do her much good to hear their thoughts as well. There is so much misery, envy, pain, malice and vanity in humans' thoughts. She reminded me the reason why I don't want to touch them.

She also said that humans ignore so many things about the world they live in. They do not know that their world is the same living organism. All forms of life in this world is like a single cell.

Every time an earthquake strikes, it's its body that shakes. When its temperature rises, i's because it's feverish. Floods are its sweat, the rain its tears, which are sometimes tears of joy or sorrow.

All of us who are the world's cells must try, though our behaviour, not to end up an infectious virus. For at some point it will ruin us in order to heal.

I realised there are similarities in the way we view humans and how humans treat us. Maybe some things are not valid only for me. This is some form of consolation.

"You used to have wings," I heard the voice inside my head. "This means you must remember what it feels like flying, no matter how deeply hidden this memory might be. You must always remember that for all those who are on the ground you're nothing but a dot in the sky. They can't touch you, harm you or contaminate you. All they can do is envy you. I have to go now. Rest assured that we will meet again...," she said and disappeared into the fog of the predawn...

I puzzled over her words. What did she knew about the period when I had wings?

I must confess I was overjoyed to have made the acquaintance of the 'White Beauty'. At the same time, I was thinking that this world would be a better place if humans, instead of envying others' beauty, tried to find their own beauty within...

9

I moved on for days, following the sunrise. The peak of a mountain hove into view. So, there was a mountain in the heart of the desert, after all. As I plodded on, I saw it hulk before me. It stood there imposing and expressionless. It seemed to be waiting for me.

I neared it even more. I was gripped by a weird feeling that I can't say was anguish. Besides, fear cannot touch me. Still, that place had a strange aura. It didn't look like any other place I had already visited.

I reached the foothills and began to ascend. At some point, I stopped short. I didn't know which direction to follow. This place looked arid and deserted. Like there was no sign of life. Like Hades' deadly breath had swept through it…

Suddenly, the earth started to shake, like a huge being trapped underneath that tried to come out. After a while, it all stopped just as inexplicably as it had begun. Silence reigned again. I couldn't account for what was going on.

I decided to continue. I had braced myself for all possibilities. As I walked on, I noticed some strange shines on the opposite slope. I turned to look in that direction. Descent was short but hard. I was nearing the spot.

When I got there, I found out it was flames. Mysterious flames gushing out of the ground. They lasted for a few moments, then disappeared. Not a single sound was heard. But there was no sense of heat either.

I stood watching that strange spectacle. At the same time, I was trying to find an explanation. Certainly, anyone else in my place would take to their heels in fright. I had to make a decision.

I looked far afield. I thought the flames formed a path, like they were trying to show me the way. I went closer and stood before the flames.

They looked rather menacing, like a fiery troop lined up. They gave me the impression that they were daring me to contend with them. To get burnt by them or mingle with them.

I thought of charging them, in hopes that I would perish. Maybe this was my one and only chance. The deathblow I had desperately been looking for.

Let's get burnt or mingle with the flames…

Flame, you are the eternal fire
the soul is made of.
Your touch purifies everything
and only in your embrace can Catharsis be attained…

Suddenly, the flames took on a form. The ones in the front looked like an arch. They formed a gate. So did the rest after a while. There were gates as far as the eye could see.

Could it be the gate that will lead to my freedom?
Is it the path that will lead me to you?
Is it time to go back where I come from?
My heart was beating fast!!!

I decided to follow this fiery path. I began to walk among the flames. For the first time, my anguish felt so sweet. I was anguished over what I would encounter at the end of the path. Perhaps the end of this road would put an end to my wanderings.

Never before had Expectation, Craving and Hope ever overwhelmed my soul in such a way. I feel them like frenzied waves lapping agains the shores of my dreams and I, like a nutshell, am at the mercy of these waves. All I have to do is see where this tempest will cast me up…

As I continued on, I heard women's voices. There was something mysterious about their tone; they sounded like otherworldly whispers, while I heard them talk in unison:

"Who's that? How dare he shatter the peace of the Ancient Ones?"

I stopped short and looked around.

I tried to figure out where these voices were coming from. I saw nothing. I continued. I've grown used to strange surprises. The women's voices, though, were heard again.

"Who's that? How dare he shatter the peace of the Ancient Ones?"

"I am Aiaibamon," I replied courageously.

"What are you here for, in the cave of the Ancient Ones?" the voices asked.

I thought for a while and replied: "I don't know where I am. I'm following the sunrise. I came here by chance."

"So, you are Aiaibamon. Nothing's accidental, Aiaibamon," the voices responded. "Come. We've been expecting you."

After these words, the voices ceased. I stood there, puzzled.

I kept walking until I came across a thick layer of fog. I couldn't see anything around me. However, this didn't stop me from plodding on. I was groping in the dark, but with great caution. As time ticked by, the veil of the fog dissipated.

I reached a dead-end. It was then that the mouth of a cave appeared before me. There was a stone plate with an inscription written in an unknown language. No doubt, this was surely the cave of the Ancient Ones the women had referred to.

I went closer to the entrance and walked in.

A relative narrow corridor started from there. On both walls, there were torches. Thanks to them, the place was lit.

I followed the corridor and came to a point where a circular space like a room formed.

In the middle stood an altar. This place was adorned with twelve huge statues. They were placed on the walls in a circular fashion. These statues were made of snow-white glossy marble. They were beautiful. They looked real, ready to move.

Never before had I seen such a thing made by human hand. No manmade work could ever compare to those statues standing before me. I stared at them with admiration for quite some time.

On their base were engraved their names. This writing, though, was unfamiliar to me. I thought this place was probably a temple. Were these the statues of the Ancient Ones? Or were they gods the Ancient Ones had made these statues for?

They looked like gods. Which gods could they be, gathered in the same place?

I sized up the place. I noticed that the corridor stretched farther away. I decided to go deeper into the cave.

After some time, I reached the end of the corridor where there was a marble plate. Slightly over it hovered a sheathed sword with a beautiful gold engraved handle. I gaped at it, dumbfounded. Behind me, I heard voices: "Welcome to the cave of the Ancient Ones..."

These voices sounded familiar to me. I turned my head to look who was behind me. What I saw was completely unexpected.

10

Three women of otherworldly beauty stood before me. Their looks showed they were not human. The strangest thing of all was that, while their voices were heard, they didn't even move their lips.

The first one had long red hair and green eyes. She wore clothes made of red leather. On her back was strapped a sheathed sword and a bow. I thought she looked like a female warrior. I was struck by her proud gaze and figure.

"I am Force," she said.

The second one had golden hair and blue eyes. She wore a light blue tunic. Around her neck hung an impressive locket with a strange symbol on it.

"I am Justice," she continued.

The third one had black hair and brown eyes. She wore a white garment. In her hand she held a dusty thick book that looked age-old. I was impressed by the ring she wore that gave off a weird shine.

"And I am Knowledge," she added.

It was plain to see. The voices I had heard earlier along the path with the flames belonged to these women. I looked at them silently, my eyes unable to hide my enthusiasm.

I decided to speak. "What place is this?" I asked.

"It's the Temple of the Immortals," they replied. "The Ancient Ones built it. They were a tribe that came here a long time ago. They were coming back from a great war. This happened in the distant past and people don't remember it anymore. Before they left again, though, they built this place to worship their gods.

"We are the Guards of the cave of the Ancient Ones. We fend off whatever could defile their temple here in the heart of Mount Baameth, the haunted mountain," they said in unison.

The haunted mountain? I felt like laughing sarcastically. Wasn't that funny?

I've been wandering around all this time to avoid what haunts me, following the sunrise. Instead of finding my own dawn, I cross paths with a haunted mountain...

I looked at the sword hovering over the plate.

"This is LightBringer," said the women. "This sword is not simply alive. It has its own soul. It also has its own judgement and will. It is dispassionate and fair. It will never take a life unless absolutely necessary. Touch it. Take it out of its sheath..."

I stood in front of the plate. I stopped short. I was irresolute for quite some time.

"Take it in your hands," they urged me. "Don't be afraid."

As soon as I touched the handle, an instant spark flooded the place. I took a step back. For a moment, I hesitantly averted my eyes, but then I decided to continue.

I held the handle again and started to unsheathe the sword. Its blade gave off a dazzling light that grew stronger.

I stared at the blade, dumbfounded. I was surprised to see various representations inside of it. This sword was really alive. All these moving images were proof enough.

Then, a strange veil of fog spread all around. Everything disappeared. I was no longer responsive to my surroundings.

I felt like I was clapping my wings. I was gripped by an unprecedented feeling. When the fog cleared, I found out I was flying high. I was really flying!!!

I looked underneath. I could see things no human eye had ever seen.

I saw otherworldly creatureawn reflection in the waters of the spirits' source...

There were other horrifying beings. It was as if they had come out of a nightmare. Their eyes were tinged with hatred. They looked menacing. Still, they couldn't harm me. I was too high for them...

I saw entire worlds come into being land others vanish.

Nothing lasts forever. Every end is a beginning, and vice versa. When a mission is accomplished, it must give place to another one.

I saw prestigious and powerful states, whose inhabitants prospered. Whatever they had was earned by dint of wisdom and prudence. Their smiling faces were full of gratitude for life.

I saw a verdant world full of trees and flowers, awash with light. It had three suns and seven moons. It reminded me of the images I had seen back in the source of the spirits, which had stirred such familiar feelings...

But I also saw poor states in dire conditions, its citizens in the slough of despond. They asked for their gods' mercy, so that they could be delivered from the impasse they had reached.

"Didn't anyone tell them that they were responsible for the state they were in?" I wondered indignantly. "We're masters of our fate. How can someone beg for help when they are not able to help themselves?"

I saw joy, bliss, beauty, but also pain, sorrow, misery. My eyes couldn't get enough if all those wondrous things I saw. I surrendered to that strange trip...

I'd love to have you here with me right now. If only I could share all these wonderful things with you. Everything looks futile without you by my side...

Suddenly, everything around me disappeared...

II

As if by magic, I reached the top of a tall rock. This rock was smooth and almost cylindrical. Its top, though, where I stood was flat.

I looked around. All I could see was a vast void. There was no way I would go down there. Only if I had my wings would I make it...

I looked around. A few yards away, I could see a bridge made of rope and planks. It was narrow. You had to poise as it was a dangerous passage.

As I cast a glance far afield, I realised that it was a long route. After some thought, I decided to check was lay on the other side. I started to cross the bridge with the utmost caution.

After a while, I heard two voices calling out simultaneously: "Come."

I stopped short.

I decided to move on. The two voices were heard again. "Come."

I carried on. I saw I was nearing the slope of another rock. There was a gate. On it was engraved a terrifying face.

I wondered what this face could possibly mean. I noticed that its mouth was an entrance. When I edged near, the gate was automatically lifted. When it opened up completely, I saw it led into a room.

The room was bright and big. The floorboard was made of a smooth shiny material that came in beautiful geometrical patterns. The room was bright because of the nuggets of gold and the colourful stones on the walls.

I walked in. I noticed there was an oval wooden table. On it were two keys. At the far end of the room, I made out a big golden crater. The flame seemed to have been burning for centuries. Behind it were two golden cages...

In each of these cages, there was a pigeon. A white pigeon in the right one, a black pigeon in the left one. I realised that the voices I had heard on the bridge came from these two pigeons.

"Come to me," said the white pigeon.

"Come to me," repeated the black one.

"If you come to me, all your dreams will come true," said the white pigeon.

"If you come to me, all your dreams will come true," repeated the black one.

I didn't know what to choose. The two pigeons spoke the same words.

After a while, though, the black pigeon spoke first: "If you come to me, I will accomplish your mission."

"If you come to me, I will give you what you need in order to accomplish your mission," said the white pigeon.

I saw a difference between what the two pigeons said. I got hold of the key on the right side. I made for the cage with the white pigeon. When I unlocked the door, it perched on my hand.

"Why did you choose me?" he asked.

"Because you give me back the freedom I just offered to you," I replied.

"That's a wise choice," said the pigeon and flew high in the sky.

"Who are you, really?" I asked.

"Who knows? Maybe I'm your soul. I'll pay you back. You should know that I keep my promises," it said and disappeared.

A new shine drenched the room. A veil of fog began to envelop me again. This time, though, I felt like I was falling. I could feel myself falling into the void for quite some time.

I realised that I got back to the same spot where I was in the beginning, holding the LightBringer. The three women were already there.

"This sword is going to be yours from now on. Listen to it when it tries to speak to you. It knows better. Only a Chosen One can use it. Only he can feel its will and speak to it..."

All this time, I had been listening to their words, but I couldn't take it anymore. Despair was devouring my lust of answers like a carnivore.

I asked the three Women if they knew who I really was and why I had ended up in this world. I asked to learn about you, if you really exist. Was your blurry image real or simply an illusion haunting me?

In vain. The answer was once again the same. All this, I had to discover by myself.

Their words, like a tempest, dashed my expectations, tearing them down the rocks of my torture once again. They didn't answer me, they didn't even tell me why I had ended up in that strange cave. The last thing they told me before they disappeared was to remember the words of my soul.

I yelled in vain with as much strength as I had left, now that my hopes had been shattered. I didn't care about any of this. All I wanted was to find out how I would go back, to learn about you, how to find you.

The three women disappeared. They vanished like the moments in the bowels of eternity. Once again, a dark void of despair spread within.

I made for the exit of the cave. I found myself in the round room with the statues. I looked at them for some time, asking for these unknown gods' help. But they looked at me silently, their faces deadpan.

Could there be life in this cold marble? Their silence spoke volumes. Yet another disappointment for me. Then, I wondered if gods are moved.

Strangely enough, I was suddenly gripped by the desire to size up the LightBringer again. I unsheathed it and held it by its handle. Its blade gave off that shine again and the sword started throbbing in my hand.

I felt the life it held once again. The ripples of its energy swept through my body. I realised that I was inside a beam of light. I put the LightBringer back in its case and everything instantly ceased.

I heard a voice inside of me say: "You have to remember you're a warrior. Don't you ever forget it."

I was to remember I'm a warrior...

I wondered what a warrior like me would do in such a world. I don't think all these woes would benefit me anymore.

At least not right now. My priority was my quest. I decided to move on. The flickering light of the torches shone on my way, until I walked out...

12

I reached the top of the hill. I waited once again for the sunrise. I was gazing at the landscape sprawling ahead, vast like my thoughts.

My gaze was fixed upon the brushstrokes left by the daylight just before it trailed off on the horizon. Then, I thought I heard a familiar sound.

It was the sound of the wind eddying. It was coming from far afield. For an instant, I thought it was the Wind that had accompanied me on the cold nights. This time, it wasn't like that...

This sound was closing in. Suddenly, I felt someone's voice laughing.

I jumped up. I grabbed hold of the LightBringer. I didn't feel it react, which was so reassuring.

"Someone who looked deep into their soul," the same voice was heard.

"Who are you?" I asked.

"You used to be a child...," the voice said.

She was swirling around me again and again, her peals of laughter unceasing.

"What do you want from me?" I shouted.

"You used to be a warrior, remember? Don't you ever forget it," the voice said again and kept swirling around me laughingly.

"A playful spirit?" I wondered. "That's what I wanted right now...Will you tell me what you want from me?" I shouted again.

The spirit kept laughing like a mischievous child and eddying. At some point, she stopped.

"Aiaibamon, calm down," the voice told me. "Only in calm waters can you see the reflection of your face. It's not me who want something from you. But you are the one who needs something from me."

"What do you mean?" I asked.

"Don't start asking the same questions," the spirit replied. "I don't have the answers you need. I can only make you see the answers you already have inside of you."

I can't say I made any sense of these words.

"I don't understand you, spirit," I said.

"Come," she said. "Don't you want to see yourself. That's what I can offer you. Do you have the courage for such a thing?"

I stopped short. Curiosity, though, trumped my inhibitions.

"I'm ready," I answered after some thought. "Spirit, you'd better make sure this is not a trap..."

The spirit's mischievous laugh was once again heard.

I saw a kind of ethereal gate forming before me. I decided to cross it...

I found myself in a weird dimly lit place. I could hardly see anything. I could hear various whispers. Otherworldly voices calling me to move on.

The landscape gradually cleared up. I saw a vast place full of mirrors. At some point, there was a big marble plate with an inscription: "Only in calm waters can you see the reflection of your face."

I remembered the spirit's words. What could that mean?

I sized up the mirrors. I suddenly began to see images I was part of. So, I saw images of my life? Things that really happened? What's this place with the three Suns and the seven Moons?

Various faces appeared, giving me familiar looks, like they knew me. What were these faces? Why were they all looking me so sadly? Why couldn't I remember anything?

The faces, like shadows, began to spin around me. This meant I had betrayed them and they were disappointed in me!!!

All the bad moments I spent in this world flashed across my mind — my failures, my mistakes, my expectations, my disappointments, my sorrows. Why do they make me feel I betrayed them, while they believed in me? What did they expect from me?

What's my past? I have no past!

Don't look at me like that as I too am betrayed!!! My own expectations betrayed me, my fate, situations, even my life itself!!!

I have so many queries. I'm looking for answers. I can't find them anywhere. I feel like crying. But even my tears betray me. They refuse to flood my soul.

All these thoughts entered my head. They keep tormenting me like the gazes of these faces...

"Stop looking at me like that!" I howled. Then, a roar was heard.

"Your self is coming...," the whispers began to say.

What looked like a monster with two heads striving to devour each other turned up. This must be my self...

One head was human wearing the helmet of a king-warrior. The other was a lion's head.

So, this is my self, eh? This is the result of my passions, miseries, disappointments, even my vanities?

Passions and vanities that, like puffs of black smoke, swirl around whoever lets them grip him, envelop him, blind him and choke him!!!

I let out a cry of indignation. I try to pull out the LightBringer. I want these shadows to disappear. I want to break the mirrors. I want everything to vanish. But the LightBringer won't get out of its case. So, this too is against me? I'm trying to unsheathe it, howling with rage, but in vain...

My eyes fell once again upon the marble plate.

"Only in calm waters can you see the reflection of your face." I felt a kind of relief amid this craze within. I turned to look at the two-headed monster.

"Stop!!!" I shouted. "Don't fight. You share the same body, the same soul. You have to learn how to coexist. You have a lot to learn from each other. You can complement each other. You can compensate for each other's weaknesses. We're one. You'll see how many things were can do if we cooperate."

The two heads stopped. They gave me a serene look and nodded. Then, they went back into the cave, disappearing through the fog. Something started to change, I could feel it!!!

The shadows stood before me again. This time, they were shooting me some calm glances, reaching out to me. I tried to touch and embrace them, but my hand pierced right through them. They weren't material. They were shadows, a dream, maybe tricks my mind played on me...

The Shadows talked to me. "Don't rack your brain," they said affectionately. "Our entire life is built on our successes, our failures and our mistakes. There is nothing inherently bad about a mistake or a failure. What is bad is for you to know it but keep repeating it. Accept that it has happened. Learn from everything. This way, you will turn your defeats into victories. You should know that these victories are even more important."

Once I said that, they disappeared through the fog. I shouted to them to come back, but they didn't respond.

I decided to follow them. I saw something that rooted me to the spot. The figure of a woman standing in the distance. She was looking at me. She wouldn't come closer. She flashed me a smile of affection, which warmed the cockles of my heart.

A while later, she went farther away. She came back holding something bright in her lap. It was a baby; I could hear its laughter. It sounded so familiar to me!!!

The woman was still standing there. I started running in her direction. She smiled at me one last time. She then turned her back. I ran after her. I was shouting at the top of my lungs, asking to know who she was.

But the female figure went away. Along with her, the baby's laughter petered out...

"Only in calm waters can you see the reflection of your face" the spirit's voice was heard.

I realised I was on top of the hill again. I didn't reply to the spirit. I was trying to figure out what had happened...

"Don't worry, Aiaibammon," continued the spirit. "He who can face himself can face everything. Farewell..."

The spirit swirled away until its mischievous laughter trailed off in the dark...

13

I was wandering about across the desert. This time, though, it was during the day. I could feel the gaze of the Sun fixed upon me. All around stretched fiery oceans of sand. I don't know why I venture into all this. Probably because there is a difference. It's the beam of light I carry within.

I'm really curious to know how this light will react to the sun of the desert. How will the sun of the desert deal with the change of my existence? I know full well how dangerous the desert is during the day. However, this was something that had to happen, sooner or later...

The heat was exhausting. The silence that reigned was quite a strain on me. It wasn't normal. I kept plodding on, nonetheless. I could feel the Sun numb my senses. Like it was trying to sap all my energy and life.

I felt like I was in a trance. I had the feeling I would lose control of my body and my mind. The only thought I was laden with was: "I will resist!!! I will resist!!!"

There were times when I could barely keep my eyes open.

It was one of those moments when you feel you're walking a tightrope towards the end, towards nonexistence.

In such a moment, I kept my eyes closed a bit longer than before. The sound of a hundred whistles, though, made me flick them open again.

I saw I was surrounded by snakes!!! Countless reptiles around me spitting venom at me. They wouldn't come closer, but they said in unison in their appalling voices:

"What are you doing in this world, Aiaibammon? Who brought you and your Thoughts here? Become one with this world, or go back where you came from. You're not wanted in this world."

I was seething with rage upon hearing their words!!! With as much strength as I had left, I unsheathed my LightBringer. I could feel its desire pierce right through me — it wanted to fight.

As I tried to ward off those reptiles, I realised our distance wouldn't change. I tried again and again, but to no avail. My rage escalated.

"You disgusting reptiles!!!" I hollered. "So, me and my Thoughts are not wanted in this world, eh? You should know that I didn't choose to be here. Until I learn why, you will have to put up with our presence, whether you like it or not. Since you can't stand our presence, come face me, otherwise go spit your venom elsewhere. Here I am, waiting for you!!! There's a word you help me recall: 'Faintheartedness'!!! Yes, that's what I call this bunch of filthy snakes like you that try to sneak into the soul in order to pour its venom. Faintheartedness wants to make the soul doubt about its purpose. To lose its faith. That's how you try to spit your venom at me from a distance. Still, you won't dare approach me..."

Against my better judgement, I blinked again, exhausted as I was. When I opened them, there was nothing there. Only sand as far as the eye could see.

What's the matter with me? What did the reptiles want? Is it likely that you bring all this upon yourself? Why is it that I feel the Serpent's betrayal on me? The Ophis. Could it be that you are the reptile, but I'm too blind to see it?

Will I feel your forked tongue if you ever touch mine? Will I feel the scales on me if I ever stroke it naked?

Will you always search to find an adorable and ostensibly innocent way to look at me, crawling next to me, every time you sink your teeth into my flesh to pour your venom?

Every drop of this venom sometimes causes me pain, and others it sears my entrails. Others still, it causes me a sense of euphoria as a side effect. But I let it flow through my veins and I'm still smiling...

So much venom was spilt into my veins that at some point I grew immune. That's what pisses you off, that's why you sent those reptiles.

You damn well know that I know. I'm sure you would say no with this alluring face of yours and your hypocritical eyes every time I point out that I know what you are. Regardless of whether I want to overlook it.

There are times when I'm overcome with so much rage that you would get scared. But you do that in such an adorable way that I don't know if this rage within will hold out much longer. If you were here beside me, maybe I would just give you a hug...

So, you're just a reptile, eh? If only you were a female Dragon! With your hot breath, you would warm my soul. What reigns inside of you, however, is the nature of the Ophis...

Days will succeed nights and moments will turn into seasons. Years will tick away and I'm sure that everyone, like me, would wonder why I still carry you inside of me.

I'm having nightmares that sound the alarm. I hear various voices in foreign languages. They're trying to warn me. Maybe it's time I extricated myself from your grip? Maybe it's time I let you go?

I was the one who let all this happen. It was my own choice, no doubt. I can't blame anyone else but me. I can't say I ever regretted anything. No, I never regretted anything. It's time I threw off the yoke of your presence inside of me...

I could simply tread on your head. You knew that. I didn't do it, though, and I won't either. But you know that as well. You should also know that your venom cannot harm me anymore!!!

It's about time you left my body and crawled where you think it's better for you. Where your venom will be effective and you can be yourself. You can't be yourself with me.

Maybe I have to bid you farewell. I'll never blame you for being forced to act according to your nature. You should know that I will keep smiling at your thought...

What am I saying? What's wrong with me? What kind of thoughts is my mind laden with? These thoughts are not mine!!!

I threw my head back. I realised that all this was a game played by the Sun of the desert. Nothing of what I saw or crossed my mind was real. Is someone or something trying to sow Faintheartedness inside of me? Is someone or something trying to give birth to Doubt within?

I stuck the LightBringer into the sand. I tried to lean my body against it. I laughed out loud. I stared at the Sun of the desert and laughingly said: "Is that it? Is that the best you could do to me?"

I rose with difficulty. I plodded on. After some time, several sounds grabbed my attention again. I raised my eyes to see a beautiful verdant landscape.

Far afield, two small waterfalls formed a lake. All I could hear was their gurgling water. There was something that drew me like a magnet. I decided to go closer. I saw a weird spectacle. A woman on the other side of the pond was kneeling down in supplication...

Her face was raised high, as if she were waiting for something, perhaps a sign or a message from the sky. Her snow-white flimsy dress — symbol of her purity — cascaded down her wheaten body.

Her emerald green eyes reflected the mantle of Spring, with all the fields, trees and flowers embroidered on it like ornaments. When she turned her gaze upon the pond, though, it was as if the blue sky was reflected in her eyes, like she had trapped in them the blue colour of the sea and all the oceans...

Her long pitch-black hair reached down to her waist and, as though windswept, it flapped and stroked the ground. It was already getting dark. The sun bidding the daylight farewell enveloped her in an orange veil.

I looked at her, stunned. Then, I mustered up the courage to go up to her. When she sensed my presence, she smiled and slowly reached out her hand. Her face looked so familiar to me...

But of course! She was the same woman I had seen in the room with the mirrors!!! I asked her for her name.

"Maira," she replied with a magic and sorrowful smile.

Maira!!! Maira!!!

Her name caressed my mind and soul. Maira means dream in the human language. Her name befitted her looks!!! Was she like a dream, or was all this just a dream?

I saw the three Suns and seven Moons again!!! Could this be my world? Was it a dream or a memory? Could you be this dream or just a memory? I feel it in my bones that you exist. I believe this with all my might. How could I ever doubt your existence?

I ecstatically closed my eyes. I felt all hope inside of me flutter its wings. My heart started thumping!!! When I opened my eyes again, though, the only thing I saw was the scorching hot sand.

I should have known better: the Sun of the desert would avenge me. I felt pain, this venomous spear pierce through my body over and over again.

I slumped to the ground and burst into sobs, but my tears wouldn't fall on the sand. The hot breath of the desert took them away...

14

Tell me...
Have you ever wondered what 'Betrayal' looks like?
I mean, if it had a form, what would it be?
This thought puzzled me many a time...
Each time, I reached a different conclusion.
The rose!!!
If Betrayal had a form,
it would look like a rose...
If you were here, you would surely give me a puzzled look. Still...
Betrayal is alluring,
just like a rose!!!
Its scent is intoxicating
and you're drawn to it, unable to react.
Just like a rose does!!!
When you reach out your hand, though,
to accept or offer it,
the result is always the same...
The bleeding wound and the pain from the thorns!!!
As it happens when someone tries to cut a rose thoughtlessly...
Are you in doubt? Still, what I say has been borne out!!!

I stood before an altar. There were four columns. When I went up several steps in the middle, I saw an embossed rose. There was an inscription as well as an old thick book gathering dust.

The writing was unfamiliar to me. I examined it on the off-chance of making any sense...

"You stand before the altar of Betrayal," I heard a voice behind me.

I turned my head and saw an elderly woman. My eyes were fixed on her.

"I am Shivi-La, the Lady of Time," she said.

I sized her up. While I was staring at her, I felt a sense of admiration. She was shrouded in an otherworldly veil of mystery. Although Time had left some deep marks on her, it hadn't yet managed to steal her allure.

She looked youthful, and so did her mannerisms. Her emerald green eyes glinted. Her rich long hair acted as a white veil over her face, which still exuded beauty.

"I am..."

"I know who you are," she interrupted me. "The book you're holding is the Chronicle of Betrayal. It says how people's Betrayal started. Do you want to know about it?" she asked me.

I nodded.

"Very well, then," she continued. "Once upon a time, a group of people fled to Urlan's desolate distant mountains. They were a bunch of fugitives and runaways. They were all thieves, murderers and robbers. The worst kind of humans. The place there was the best natural refuge. No one would ever track them down there. They settled down and gradually made an organised society. With the passage of time, they became a more cohesive society and started to get to know the secrets of the place. They explored the multiple caves in the area. They reached places inside the bowels of the earth. There, they met the Everons, a subterranean tribe of human-like demons. After they came in contact with them, they allied and mingled. The Everons once lived on the surface. Their heart was insatiable, filled with hatred for humans. They blame gods for doing them wrong. They insulted them by giving humans a soul, while they had none. They consider themselves a superior species. That's why they disdain humans for having a soul. In the distant past, the Everons waged war against humans. They always wanted to wipe us out and dominate the world. They think that this will be the best revenge against gods. Faced with this great danger, all human races united. It was time for the big battle. A fierce clash took place. Thanks to their mental strength and hope, humans defeated them. With gods' help and support, they achieved a great victory. The Everons, humiliated, were ousted. Harbouring even more hatred now, they retreated into the bowels of the underworld. They have been in there ever since, waiting for humankind to wither away, so that they can lash back when the opportunity presents itself. By building huge gates made of copper, humans sealed every exit they knew led to the underworld..."

"I'm sure they thought of these people as a great opportunity to this end," I interrupted her.

"It's true. This group of people had similar pursuits. They were trying to come up with a way to go back to human society. They knew this would be really hard without getting persecuted. They didn't just want to go back; they wanted to dominate! At some point, one of them, Am-Avar, had an incredible plan. He thought that the best way to achieve their goal was to exploit all kinds of spiritual and metaphysical concerns. They knew full well that it was something that struck terror and awe into people's hearts. They would return to human societies dressed up as priests. They would try to convince humans that gods themselves spoke to them. As humans' bad nature couldn't change, there was a plan B as well...They themselves were ruthless and didn't believe in anything. He suggested spreading out across all the kingdoms. Wherever they went, they picked up a god to 'serve'. They would try to draw in as many people as they could. They would put out all the stops to gain financial power. They would try to earn the favour of the powers that be, so as to gradually influence decision-making. With the passage of time, some 'wise men' would appear, installed by them. With their writings and speeches, they would support them and distort all kinds of real knowledge. They would cut people off from their past and memories. Finally, they would all be united under a single religion and fraternity. Without any rush, taking slow but steady steps, they would conquer the world. That's what happened. They spread everywhere. They turned up as priests, thinkers, even merchants, while some of them as ostensible defenders of lay persons. They poisoned the world with their phoney sermons, posing false dilemmas and sowing disorientation. They fomented fanaticism and hatred among humans. They intimidated everyone, invoking gods' purported wrath. They created fake threats, so as to take advantage of human fear. People would believe they needed their protection. They made people not think freely. They made them feel they depended on them. For optimal results, they used the 'whisper of oblivion', a secret they had learnt from their subterranean allies. It was a buccina that, thanks to a magic spell, blew people's minds, clouding their judgement. They had one in each temple and sounded it three times a day. They were supposed to summon their believers to the temple. This way, they slowly and steadily eradicated all clear thinking and prudence. He who had a different opinion was presented as acting against gods' wish and they made sure he was slandered, mocked and reviled — backed up by the phoney wise men. No other kind of knowledge was allowed but the one they imposed. They presented everything in their own way. Thus, they gradually influenced the powers that be. They themselves were too cowardly to become warriors, so they sowed dissension. They turned one kingdom against another to the bitter end. They had control and power. They brought death, pain and disaster in the name of the gods..."

"All this is so scary, old woman," I said, surprised. "Didn't humans realise any of this, so as to resist?"

"My dear Aiaibammon," she replied, "the mob acts like a child. It always needs someone to hold its hand and lead it to prudence. A child is spontaneous, immature and impressionable. It needs the right kind of advice and guidance. Only this way will it find its own path, sooner or later. Take this crystal ball and look inside."

I hesitantly held the ball in my hands and did as I was told. I started seeing images. At first, they were blurry but, as seconds ticked away, they became clearer.

When these images cleared up, a sense of horror filled me. What I saw was like it had sprung from the worst nightmare a human mind could conjure up.

I saw weird states with tall buildings that hid the sun. These buildings were so repulsive, like the figments of a sick imagination. I wondered whose sick mind could have ever created what I saw...

There was no ground, only a hard flat material like a soft colourful stone. There was no trace of earth or trees, while a menacing black cloud was wandering across the sky.

I suddenly saw herds of metal beasts!!!

They had two round eyes that gave off a weird light, while every now and then they let out some hair-raising cries. Inside their bellies were human creatures holding what looked like round trays. Still, these human beings didn't seem to have been devoured. All this huge flock was following a specific course.

I saw countless human creatures like the ones I met in this world. They were all dressed in strange clothes much akin to uniforms. The man wore a kind of lead, probably for their master's hand...

Their faces stern, they were walking swiftly and in order, like they were running to catch up with something. They didn't look around. They didn't care about who was next to them. Only a few times they exchanged some glances of envy, disdain, suspicion and scorn.

I could make out some demons, their bodies made of metal. They were extremely tall and slender, with three luminous eyes. One was over the other. The eye on top was red, the one in the middle orange and the lower one green, flickering at intervals.

It was them who ordered the human creatures and the metal beasts to move. These humans and metal beasts must have been captives or slaves. All this can't have been made by them. Still, I couldn't but marvel at their chief, who imposed such discipline on them.

All this can't have been the creation of free people!!!

Otherwise, wouldn't they have done something to see the sunrise and the sunset, the moon and the stars?

They surely missed the trees, the flowers, the rustling of the leaves, the sounds of the forest, the rivers and the chirps of the birds.

Only prisons could be built in this way. That's what they seemed to be: prisons. I saw that these human creatures lived in small square cages. However, they allowed them to live in families.

The strange thing was, they weren't locked. They could get in and out of their cells at will. But this didn't make any difference. All that place was a huge prison. These cells seemed to be places where they could rest after their laborious work.

A while later, I saw who ruled that place. In every cell, there was a fiendish creature the shape of a box with two horns. These must have been their supervisors. They looked so ghastly!!!

The demons' faces took on the form of a human issuing commands. He told them what to do, what to believe, what to consider right and wrong — everything!!!

The human beings were pinned to the ground in front of them. They simply carried out their orders. They were so disciplined, they obeyed on the spot.

However, apart from human, these demons took on other forms as well.

I saw huge metal birds flying in the sky, breathing fire down to the ground, spreading death.

These metal beasts seemed to have trunks or what looked like a horn on the forehead. They destroyed everything in their path. Soldiers with strange spears that could kill from a distance.

People of different colours suffering. Little children emaciated, sick and helpless...

Scenes of horror!!!

What kind of creatures were they, finding it so easy to wreak havoc?

How could they be so ruthless? Had they developed only the art of Death and destruction, pain and misery, sorrow and despair?

How had they so cruelly subjugated everything around them? Where did these demons come from? Couldn't anyone resist them? Were they so powerful?

I let out a cry of indignation. "I don't want to see anything else!!! I want to het away from here!!!"

I realised I was standing before an elderly woman. I was holding the crystal ball in fright. Then, she came up to me and snatched it from my hands. I looked on in horror, unable to utter a single word.

"This will happen if Betrayal reigns...," she said knowingly and disappeared...

15

It was a few hours before dawn. Loyal to my peregrinations, at the mercy of my unknown route, I reached a strange place.

The Wind and the Night were singing in hushed tones to the Moon. I was listening out for the song until I saw a rock. I though it would be a nice place to rest.

I had been sitting there for some time when a strange sound caught my attention. It sounded like a sigh, but it can't have been human.

I felt the earth shake under my feet; maybe it was an earthquake. I jumped up to protect myself.

I heard that weird sound again...

I turned to look. I saw the rock shake. It wasn't an earthquake, after all. Something else had happened. After a while, the rock stopped moving. I saw what looked like a human figure in the dark.

I unsheathed my LightBringer. It didn't feel any threat, which reassured me. Surprised as I was, I heard the rock say:

"Don't be afraid, traveller. I won't harm you."

"What kind of creature are you?" I asked in surprise.

"I'm a Golem," it replied. "You can't be a human to me either, although you look like them."

"That is true," I said to the weird creature. "I'm not a human either."

"I'd be interested to hear your story, traveller. Maybe you want to hear mine. We have a long time at our disposal until dawn breaks."

"Yes, I'd love to hear your story," I said. "What will happened at dawn?"

"I'll explain everything to you, traveller," said the Golem. "This is my story... I'm made from stone and clay. A very long time ago, a wizard made me, so that I would serve him. The one who created me breathed life into me, thanks to his magic. Still, I have no soul. No one else knew about me. My existence was out of bounds to the other humans. As I'm sure you know, Time wears people out. At some point, they come to an end. When my creator sensed that he was nearing his end, he asked me to leave. I should hide, he said, as no one was to find out about my existence.

He was afraid that they might try to destroy me. You surely know that humans are hostile towards what they do not know."

"More than you can imagine," I interrupted the Golem.

While I was listening to the creature, I felt appalled by the idea that I could be such a creature myself.

No, this couldn't be true. I have a soul, I heard her, I spoke to her!!!

What is a soul, though?

I've heard of a wise man who said that the soul is the essence of a divine breath trapped in a body. Others say that the body is the one that protects the soul.

When the soul leaves the body, it is ablaze so as to purge all the impure parts. Then, it goes back to the star it belongs to.

So, does each soul belong to a star? What could be my star? Is the place I come from a star?

Are there pure and impure souls? Isn't actions that are characterised as pure and impure? Is it impure actions that show that a soul is missing?

"I chose these places to hide," the Golem continued, interrupting my thoughts, "because nobody comes here. The vast swamps are nearby. These swamps are dangerous. Humans avoid it. Still, there's another reason, which I discovered just after I arrived here. Butterflies..."

"Butterflies?" I asked.

""Butterflies are small winged and colourful creatures," answered the Golem. "Haven't you ever seen one?"

I shook my head. "No, never."

"They're beautiful," he carried on. "I've heard stories about them and that they live only for one day. Many people say that eacb butterfly is a soul. They also say that many human souls that have died go back to Earth in the form of butterflies only for one day…As you see, traveller, here I've found my freedom and a safe refuge. Every dawn, I go find the butterflies. I become one with them. As I don't have a soul, at least I feel great to be among souls. You never know. Maybe one of them will sneak into me and I'll get my own soul. Till then, as long as they fly around me or sit on me, they'll add beauty and colour to my body. Every day, I wake up before dawn to go find them."

At first, I felt like laughing.

I was resting on top of a living rock until it snapped out of its sleep and I mistook that for an earthquake. Then came its yawns, which were the strange sounds I had heard. This rock then proved to be some weird creature that was now telling me its story…

I have to admit that its words almost moved me to tears as it dawned on me that we had so much in common.

I don't know if I was supposed to feel better just because someone was in the same state as I was. No, I wouldn't wish that on anyone, not even my enemy.

I began to narrate my own story to the Golem that seemed to touch it in the same way as its story touched me.

It was happy to have been given the chance to exchange some words with someone else as the freedom and beauty it had found in that place weren't able to offset the loneliness it felt.

But it was getting late and dawn began to break…

"Come. It's time," the Golem said and led me somewhere not very far from a green clearing. "They will be here in a while," it whispered when we stopped. "Wait and see."

It was right. No sooner had it uttered these words than the butterflies turned up. A beautiful eddy, a riot of colours, was coming towards us.

Once again, it was one of those magical moments that are becoming a rarity. Every time I think of it, I wonder how people can let magic fade away in their world.

"Come with me," the Golem shouted.

I followed it and we entered this whirlwind. We became one with the butterflies that were countless. I couldn't put into words the beauty I saw or the feelings it stirred up inside of me.

I couldn't get my fill of them. Their touch made me feel like a wound was being healed within.

If only you were here with me!!!

Why aren't you here with me to share this moment with you?

I'd love to see you inside this colourful eddy made of butterflies. I couldn't imagine a better ornament for you than this vortex around you like a colourful mantle...

The memory of you saddened me for a while. It also reminded me that I had to carry on with my wandering. I had to leave. Nothing, no matter how beautiful, can last forever.

The only thing that is eternal is you!!!

I carried on. The Golem pleaded with me not to tell anyone about its existence. I had no reason to deny that. I glad to hear that I would always be welcome to his refuge.

In some respects, I envied the Golem. It had found some things all of us need.

It had found a safe shelter as well as colour and beauty in its life. But was it true?

One could say that it found an illusion of all this and it built a golden prison around it...

But there are some people who prefer to take a step forward, choosing to fight and take risks.

There are some people who choose to be inert. I'm not the one who will judge the Golem's choices. In our life, we often encounter crossroads.

Some other times, we stand still and indecisive before them, dithering.

Other times, we make a choice and move on. The outcome always decides which choice is the right one...

Just like the Golem, I myself have built a safe refuge around me. Were I in its place, I would seek my own soul, my own beauty and colour.

The attempt alone at pursuing them would make me feel better about myself. Even if all my choices proved wrong.

After all, in my own eyes, even the illusion of what surrounded the Golem looks so futile.

It chose to hide, yet isn't it its isolation that keeps it from sharing what it built around it?

What's the point of everything if one cannot share it or even present it? If one doesn't show everyone that it belongs to one?

At any rate, I won't judge you, Golem. We are our choices. These are decided by the outcome or at least by how hard we fought for them.

Not everyone's the same. Each one of us chooses and does what he or she deems to be better. What I will glean from our brief encounter is the beauty and the colour. What all of us need so badly!!!

I needed colour and beauty after Betrayal's nightmarish vision...

16

Time was unfolding his mantle. Every time the hours and moments flapped on him, days gave place to nights, and the other way round. There were so many alternations. At some point, I came across some ruins.

This place looked desolate. It was evident that it had succumbed to some great catastrophe. People once lived here, yet there was no trace of them anymore...

Far afield, I saw a huge wall that, every time I looked at it, gave me the impression that it was one of the edges of the world. I wondered again and again what could lie behind it...

I wandered around the ruins, trying to figure out what could have happened. With time, I had the feeling that I wasn't alone...

It was getting dark. At some point, various sounds shattered the silence. I realised that I was surrounded by a group of people training their weapons on me.

I grabbed hold of my LightBringer, waiting for their next move. We exchanged some mute glances.

For some strange reason, the LightBringer was calm. It felt no threat, yet I was thinking that I had to brace myself.

This carried on for quite some time, until one of them said: "He doesn't seem to be one of them. Hang on a minute. I'm sure I know you..."

The man who spoke came closer. Then, I recognised him. It was Shira-Tuth, that smiling boy I had met at that river long before. He had changed. Still, along with his male characteristics, he still retained that shine on his face.

"Yes, Shira-Tuth, we do know each other," I replied. "A long time ago, you shared with me that fire on the banks of a river. You played one of your beautiful melodies. You had just got your name if you remember..."

That familiar smile of his alighted on his face.

"This voice and looks are surely familiar to me. Pyr-Kaa!!!" he exclaimed after several seconds and ran to hug me. "It's really you!!! How could I ever forget that mysterious stranger I met on the most important day of my life? The day I had passed that bravery ritual. Sorry to welcome you like that. As you've already realised, we're in a dire condition..."

The other humans with him put their guns down with relief.

I asked him what was going on. He said we would have time to get my questions answered. But, first, he would have to introduce me to Kron-Ammoth, their chief...

I cracked a smile when I saw that the red horse with the golden mare was still with him. I remembered its name: Gror (meaning 'Thunder').

Shira-Tuth mounted Gror and made for the big wall. The others followed on foot. On our way there, I saw two huge statues scattered among the ruins. I couldn't understand what they represented. Not even they hadn't been spared the disaster.

Of course, they couldn't compare to what I had seen in the cave of the Ancient Ones. Yet, they still bore the marks of their former grandiosity.

I asked someone next to me about the forms of the statues. He answered that these forms belonged to Namar and Aramos, the two gods that were worshipped in Len-Bion.

Namar explained to me that it was like a bright god protector of life and fertility. They offered him cereals and fruit, so that he would bless the harvest and their lives. Their children would grow up naturally and all their activities would flourish.

Aramos was something like a dark god. He was the one who brought balance and justice. He transported the souls to the underworld. They sacrificed animals in order to propitiate him, so that he wouldn't wreak havoc with the crops, the herds and nature in general.

The first one was depicted as wearing a golden suit of armour that was like the sun, as they explained to me, but it was also represented on his shield. The same held for his sword handle that was engraved with an eagle's leg.

The second one was represented in a bright but pitch-dark suit of armour. His helmet was emblazoned with a bat's wings. As for his sword handle, it was black ending in a dragon's foot.

They considered them both ultimate warriors. They believed that it was their clash and co-existence that balanced existence.

"Something like Order and Chaos," I thought to myself. "I doubt if people, who have an extraordinary knack for confounding ideas, know the real meaning of these notions."

Each god had his own priests. Namar's priests were the Aquai, while those of Aramos were the Mahakwe. When I asked who ruled this place, they told me about the Senate, which was the council of the seven old priests. As the Aquai were the older ones, after the advent of the Mahakwe this council consisted of three Aquai and three Mahakwe, led by an archpriest of the former.

They also told me that, in the past, Len-Bion was riddled with the civil strifes of its factions, until some old men took a peacekeeping initiative.

Fortunately for Len-Bion's inhabitants, the old men's wisdom prevailed. The factions reconciled. Since then, the Senate has been in charge of the governance. This was a tribute to the those old men who managed to bring peace. From then on, days and years flitted by quietly and in harmony.

I found out that Kron-Ammoth, the one I met, was a wise old man, an Aquai archpriest of Namar, that is at the helm of the Senate.

As we walked on, we continued to talk and I looked around. I could feel my soul constrict as my eyes fell on the ruins. After a while, it started to drizzle. It was as if the sky had overflown with the entire world's tears of sorrow.

We walked for quite some time until we got to a point where Shira-Tuth was waiting for us.

When we approached him, he asked me to follow him. We headed together for that huge wall I had seen from a distance.

"This wall looks like it's the edge of the world," I said to Shira-Tuth.

"It is in some way," he replied.

I gave him a puzzled look.

"I'm sure you're wondering what I mean," he carried on. "Kron-Ammoth will explain everything to you. After what happened, he gave orders that we present stranger to him. I'm sure he has his reasons. I hope you don't mind."

I nodded my head in assent. Then, we plodded on...

17

After a while, we reached the spot where the old man, plunged in thought, sat on a rock. He was gazing at the horizon, his chin resting on his fist.

When we went closer, Shira-Tuth didn't have the time to announce our coming. The old man, his eyes staring at the ground, said: "Welcome, stranger. Shira-Tuth has told me about you. You have known each other for a long time, it seems."

"It's true," I replied. I returned his greeting and asked him what was going on.

The old man looked at me and shook his head with consternation.

"I think it is plain to see that we're facing some serious problems. Tell me about yourself, stranger," he continued. "I sense something weird about your presence. Would you like to tell me what brought you to these places?"

"I once decided to follow the sunrise," I answered.

"To follow the sunrise...," repeated the old man. "Why would you do such a think?" he asked.

I shrugged my shoulders. "To be frank, I don't know," I answered.

"I see," said the old man. He then pensively brought his hand to his beard, while nodding to the others around us to leave.

When we were left alone, he turned to look at me and it was then that I saw his face clearly for the first time.

"You're not here by chance, stranger," said Kron-Ammoth.

I was puzzled. "What do you mean, nestor?"

"I feel something about you that is not human. Tell me, stranger, who are you? Is your advent a good or a bad omen?"

I decided to be frank with him. I had no reason not to be.

He was human, but I felt there was something different about him too, just like when I met Shira-Tuth. Maybe humans in these places were completely different.

The more I observed his face, the more I got the impression that I knew him from somewhere. But where? He looked so familiar to me. He made me trust him. Never before had a human made me feel like this.

I resolved to narrate my story, this riddle with all the missing pieces that I keep searching for.

Once again, I began to talk about the darkness inside of me, my questions regarding my origins, my wanderings, even the things that haunted me. I also spoke to him of you and your calling...

I told him about the strange places and creatures that I met, even the humans — what I saw and thought of them...

As I spoke, the old man listened to me intently. He didn't look surprised. Every now and then, he would nod in comprehension, even when the night wind tousled his long snow-white hair.

His gaze was still piercing, yet different. Maybe because he no longer had any misgivings about me.

Many times during his narration, he gave me the impression that he could barely stifle a smile. But why would he do that? How can someone smile upon hearing someone else's suffering? I must have been seeing things...

When I was done, he once again put his hand on his white beard and told me:

"I'm sorry to have heard all this, stranger. I see you're following your own path of suffering that seems to make you or break you."

"Up until now, my path has been the sunrise, until I find my own Sunrise," I concluded.

Kron-Ammoth cracked a faint smile. He then lowered his gaze to the grind and took to poking the soil with his long wooden cane.

"If only I had solutions and answers to your ordeal, stranger," he said in a low voice.

Still, he knew more. I felt that more intensely as we talked.

"As far as humans are concerned," he said, "although I can't say you're wrong, you'd better learn a few things about them, so as to form an opinion. Perhaps from now on, you won't be so judgemental towards them."

"What do you mean?" I asked.

"I'll tell you a story, as it was narrated to me when I was a child," he explained. Kron-Ammoth's words piqued my interest.

"I'm all ears," I said.

"When Life was created," the old man began, "Time, like a newborn baby, took its first tentative steps. It was back then when darkness reigned. God Creator summoned His gods creations and asked them to do something for Him as darkness was cold and colourless with no beauty. The gods responded that they would be happy to grant His wish. However, they asked Him why He didn't want to do it Himself, since it would be far easier for Him. Only a thought of His would be enough and each of His creations would be unrivalled and incomparable to their own.

God Creator then explained to them that, if He were to do that, every one of His creations would carry part of His Essence, like He did with them.

So, they had to do it themselves. This way, every creation would have a flow and continuity in Time, forming a constant perennial circle.

The gods understood what God Creator meant. In order to carry out His wish, they decided to create beauty.

In order to do so, the gods decided to create worlds and creatures to inhabit them, using various ornaments as material. The gods took Light, Fire, Wind and Water, even the green colour of nature, and began to decorate everything around them...

God Creator was very pleased with the gods' work. That's why He sent His Word everywhere through His Spirit, so as to express His gratification. So, everything contained the Breath of God Creator.

At the same time, the gods' work vexed the creatures of Darkness as it made them lose their sovereignty. From then on, they seized the opportunity to take revenge on the gods and God Creator.

The last word created by the gods was Gaia-Chthon. When the gods started creating it, they soon discovered that there was too little Light and Fire left to complete it. Sad as they were, they tried to find a way as they couldn't leave this world incomplete.

Then, they thought of making a heart with the remaining Fire and put it in the middle of Gaia-Chthon. The little Light, they placed around it, forming the sky. They also used plenty of Water, Wind and a lot of soil for the ground...

They made humans out of dust and water. That's what they called the creatures that would inhabit Gaia-Chthon. Still, these creatures were very weak and their bodies couldn't live for a long time. That's why the gods resolved to give them a precious gift that would offset their weakness. This gift was Soul and Hope.

The Soul is made of the Celestial Fire, the rarest material the gods possessed. Hope was what would always give them strength, so as not to give up on their goal.

While the Celestial Fire simmered inside man, his soul would be alive. Along with hope, he would have the chance to extricate himself from the clay and reach the Light, living for eternity.

The gods instilled Imagination in them, so that they would have a glimpse of the world of Light for as long as they remained in their weak bodies."

"So, that's how the fight between the humans and the Everons began...," I interrupted Kron-Ammoth's narrative.

"That's right," replied Kron-Ammoth. "They were in their crosshairs as a creation of the gods. But I see you already know about that. That's humans...

Still, something else is said. While humans were being made, an assistant of the gods secretly took from them some material and tried to create his own humans. The end result were soulless creatures. At some point, the gods discovered that and punished him severely.

As for your Sunrise, which you seek, think that maybe you're not here by chance. Maybe your destiny has in store for you a role that not even you can imagine."

Then, he turned to ask me: "Do you really believe in destiny?"

I didn't quite understand what he expected me to reply. I shook my head to show how ignorant I was.

"You know, there are some people who believe that what happens is what is meant to happen. Not even the gods themselves can avoid destiny. No matter how much one deviates in life, one always comes back to the same path.

There are some who believe that man has free will and choice in selecting his path. Every human being, with his choices and actions, can determine his own destiny.

There is a third view, according to which destiny is at work, but what man can do is choose the path that will lead him to it. In other words, his actions and choices will determine how fast or slowly, how easy or hard he will find it to get there."

Kron-Ammoth's words got me thinking. For the first time, I learnt that this world was called Gaia-Chthon.

"What you told me is wise and useful," I said, interrupting my thoughts. "However, I see no role that I could play here. I can't understand what you could possibly need me for. You look strong people with courage, stubbornness, determination and patience. I'm sure that, sooner or later, you will build it all from scratch."

"Look around you," he said. "What you see is the work of the Mahakwe. They appeared here out of nowhere long ago. They presented themselves as priests of our god Aramos. I don't know if you've heard of Him and what we believe in."

"I had the chance to learn a few things about your gods," I said, nodding my head.

The Old Man continued: "All the people here, especially the Aquai, welcomed them. We were never leery or hostile towards them. We think every god is like a father. We humans are their sons and daughters. No child has the exclusive privilege to be the only one loved and honoured by his or her parents. Of course, parents must not discriminate against their children. Something wasn't quite right about them. At first, they were aloof and began to neglect their duties. Then, they secretly met one another. In the end, their behaviour changed. They became hostile. They were arrogant and disdainful. Like they had achieved their goal and were powerful. People started to react. With the passage of time, they demanded that he Senate do something about it. After a while, there appeared some supposedly wise men, who defended them. They mocked whoever spoke ill of them. People began to chafe. But it was my fault too. I should have realised earlier how serious the problem was. So, I called a summit. Still, they refused to participate. Saying that, since they formed the majority along with the Aquai, whatever the Senate's resolution might be, it couldn't be regarded as fair and impartial. It was patent that something was not right; they were up to something. How else could such a reaction be explained? Never before had they treated the Senate in such a way. I told them they had no other choice. It was time to shed light on the case. That night, though, there broke out a series of explosions in buildings, temples and libraries. That's what all these ruins are. The next morning, as we estimated the extent of the damage, we realised that the Mahakwe and their men had abandoned Len-Bion. We never found out what their purpose or plan was."

I realised why they had welcomed me like that. When they saw me, they surely took me for a spy or a man of the Mahakwe...

What I heard sounded so familiar to me. "Like they're part of Betrayal," some of my thoughts were heard.

"So, you know about her," I heard the old man's surprised voice.

I nodded and told him about that small temple I stumbled upon, with the altar featuring the engraved rose. I told him about the strange elderly lady, Shivi-La, with her crystal ball, where I saw so many harrowing images..."

"You met Shivi-La?" the old man interrupted me again. "I happen to know her very well, but this is the first time I've ever heard about this temple you mentioned."

"Shivi-La is a solitary and strange person wandering around Len-Bion's wilderness. She rarely appears where humans live."

"I don't find it strange," I thought. I realised, though, that the story Kron-Ammoth recounted regarding the creation of humans and their strange world made me change my opinion of them.

"The crowd can avoid her wherever they see her," the old man carried on. "Everyone can believe she's a crazy witch. But nothing could be further from the truth...When Shiva-La was little, she ended up on the banks of a river. Then, a female figure turned up before her. She promised to give her the gift of insight, on condition no man ever touched her. You know, much earlier than Shivi-La, I found out about the existence of Betrayal for the first time. She had warned me. Still, she hadn't told me what she told you. Nor had she ever shown me her ball, so as to look inside. What she did show me, however, was how to read the stars. She said that, whatever might be true of destiny, a small part of it is written in them. It's been a long time since I last saw her...I've recently read the stars. They revealed to me that some big and stunning things will happen. I couldn't discern anything more than that. They also told me that someone would arrive. That's why I asked every newcomer to be brought to me. As soon as I sensed your presence, I realised it was you they told me about. You're not here by accident — this, I can vouch for. For Shivi-La to have entrusted you with all this, she must have had some very serious reasons. She knows something. Her words are not to be derided. Whatever she has said has been borne out. But there is something else you need to know," Kron-Ammoth continued.

Voices suddenly rent the air. Noises and loud cries interrupted his words. We both listened out to check what was going on. Two people gasping for air and unable to catch their breath ran towards us. One of them whispered something in his ear.

"When did that happen?" Kron-Ammoth raised his voice in surprise.

"A few hours ago," the other man replied.

Kron-Ammoth leapt to his feet and made for the crowd. We followed behind him. There was a commotion and all you could see were people running scared and letting out some cries of despair. Then, Kron-Ammoth began to ask some people to come closer and issued orders. Then, they ran in different directions.

I could hear him say that they shouldn't panic. They were to tell the crowds that they must all stay at home until further notice. To others, he said they had to spread the news of the imminent danger, and those men in Len-Bion who could hold a gun had to assemble at that spot.

What made quite an impression on me was that he commanded all the metal workers to amass as much copper as they could. They were to make it red-hot and keep it in the form of a liquid.

At some point, we locked gaze.

"A huge troop of subterraneans are coming here," he said. "This means that the gates have cracks. They have found some ways out. We have to stop them. As for the story I was telling you, we'll pick up where we left off some other time when conditions are more favourable."

"Why did you ask the metal workers to melt copper?" I asked.

"Before this humankind and a long time ago, there lived in Gaia-Chthon a human race that was superior to this one. They were a generation of heroes. Some claimed that they were gods' heirs. This species made three crusades in distant places of this world. They crushed the Everons and every subterranean race. It was they who sealed them with the copper gates, so that they would never come to the surface again. The blood of this humankind contained copper, while it turned out that the subterraneans have a soft spot for copper. That's why they made the gates out of this material. Spreading copper on the blades of the swords and arrows or spears would prove beneficial during the battle against them."

"What do contemporary humans have in their blood?" I asked, impressed by Kron-Ammoth's erudition.

The old man smiled. "Iron," he replied. "They have iron in their blood. That's why they often become oxidised. It is this that erodes their bodies. If only they could replace iron with…"

"What's this oxidisation? How do you know all this? Do I have such a thing too?" My thoughts and queries overwhelmed me.

"Pyr-Kaa," Kron-Ammoth interrupted my thoughts, while giving me some knowing looks. "You think you have to wonder if you came here by chance? These moments call for actions, not words. Our men will need someone to lead them to the battle. Someone who will instil in them bravery, faith, courage, strength, trust. Seeing your sword, I gather you're not only a warrior but something much greater than that. You are the one who must lead. Will you do that? Don't forget that whatever happens in this world directly affects you as well…"

I stopped short for a few seconds. The old man was right. Whatever will happen in this world will directly affect me. The same holds for my wanderings. I would never let anyone or anything stop it or ruin it. Nobody and nothing would keep me away from you!!!

"I'll do it," I stated with resolve. "Let's wait for the men to gather," I added, upon which the old man smiled and nodded his head.

18

The time had arrived. The procession set off. Len-Bion's earth shook under the horse hooves. Two thousand horsemen, one thousand foot soldiers and two thousand archers managed to gather.

All of them were Len-Bion's best warriors and lots of laymen who had bravely responded to the call of this battle. Its outcome would decide the future or even the lives of these people.

It was so touching to see how Len-Bion' men had responded, bearing in mind that everyone knew they were bound to die and never come back.

The tracers reported that the huge army of the monsters, which looked endless, had set up camp on the Flatland of Ankhammon. We had to flit. This place wasn't very far from Len-Bion.

We set out silently. A huge crowd had gathered, all looking sad, wondering if they should bid us farewell one more time. We walked away and, after a gruelling course that lasted several hours, we reached the hills, just before the spot where the enemy lay.

The night was falling. We could make out fires in the enemy's camp that went as far as the eye could see.

I heard the rustle of leaves being trampled. I looked back and saw Shira-Tuth and Kron-Ammoth. They seemed to have been there with me for a long time, although I hadn't sensed their presence.

"Is everything alright?" I asked, my eyes falling on Shira-Tuth.

"Yes," he answered. "Our men have set up camp, waiting for orders. I think you have realised that we stand no chance. Maybe we'll be able to hold them up for a while."

"Do you believe we should send for someone to Len-Bion to tell people to leave?" I asked.

"Maybe it's a good idea," he replied.

"There are times," Kron-Ammoth interrupted us, "when you realise whatever happened in the past happened so that someone might be led to the specific place in the specific time. That's what's happening now. Each one of us, though our own path, ended up here. That's what matters. No matter the outcome, there are those who blaze trail and those who follow them. Never forget that..."

I felt like laughing. The path I carved leads me to my death in an alien world, taking part in a battle that I can say is not mine.

I was struck by Kron-Ammoth's sangfroid. He didn't look scared at all.

Dawn was breaking. I could see a flurry of activity in the opposite camp. The enemy was preparing for battle.

"Our men are waiting for orders," I heard a voice. It was one of the knights.

"You will soon have them," I replied. He went back to our men.

I spent some time gazing at the enemy's camp. They looked like a huge army of ants. They were still moving to brace themselves for battle.

I had mixed feelings. I felt like the outcome of the battle rebounded on me. This was such an unbearable burden. Then, my LightBringer started to shine. I felt it wanted to speak to me.

I placed my hand on the handle, clutching it. I began to see images. When all this was done, I called out Shira-Tuth. "Here's what we're going to do," I told him in a strict and resolute tone. He stared at me intently.

"We'll be the first ones to attack," I said, my eyes sparkling. He gave me a puzzled look.

"But that's sheer suicide!" he faltered.

Kron-Ammoth eyed me curiously. In the end, he smiled knowingly. It seemed that he realised or already knew something that I wasn't privy to. That's what I gathered from his deadpan expression.

"Yes, we'll attack them first," I repeated, my voice sounding more certain now. "Listen how we're going to do it. We'll slowly climb down the hill. The horsemen will lead the way, followed by the foot soldiers and the archers farther back. You see how they're arrayed? We're going to strike in the middle. We'll charge them. If we manage to break into the forefront in the middle, their rear part will try to surround us. The foot soldiers will protect the horsemen sidewards. The archers will hit whoever comes behind us. Since I have no horse, I'll lead the foot soldiers."

"But that will be really dangerous for you," interrupted Shira-Tuth.

"I don't think my life costs more than anyone else's around us. All our men here followed us just as bravely, knowing their end. Why don't you go inform them now?"

He silently obeyed, making for the place where our men were.

After a while, our men were arrayed for battle. When Shira-Tuth explained my plan to them, they gave me silent looks.

"Men of Len-Bion," I shouted at the top of my lungs, "you're here right now because, although you are very few in number, you are the bravest of humans. Neither the numbers of the enemy nor death itself scared you. The fate of your families depends on us right now. Even if all of us breathe our last here, there will be more who will be inspired by our example. This alone makes us winners. Let's move on to the battlefield to make our own history in eternity."

The men raised their weapons and yelled. In a while, we slowly went down the hill in military formation. The horsemen led the way, behind them followed the foot soldiers and further behind was Shira-Tuth with the archers.

Following my orders, the archers stood in the middle of the hill. The horsemen and the foot soldiers were marching towards the enemy slowly but steadily and with resolve.

As we drew near, I could make out their army. It was made up of monsters. No one knew where they really came from. Could they be the result of some blasphemous magic?

Upon seeing them, I remembered what Kron-Ammoth had told me about the one who had stolen material from the gods and made his own soulless creatures. I even recalled the Golem, which was a concoction looking for a soul.

Do these creatures have a soul? If they don't, do they know it? Do they know that, when their body stops moving, no star will be waiting for them? How do they feel for their creator, knowing all this? What is it that determines their actions? Do they have a judgement and a will of their own? What is it like not having a soul? How many soulless creatures in the form of humans walk among people without the latter knowing it?

At some point, all these horrible questions were interrupted by a figure I saw; he must be their leader. Unlike the rest, he seemed more like a human, although he looked humongous.

He was riding a black horse. He wore a pitch-black shiny suit of armour. I was impressed by his helmet and sword handle — they were both made of black metal. His helmet was emblazoned with a bat's wings, while a dragon's foot was engraved into the sword handle.

I was so upset!!! That's how the people of Len-Bion represented Aramos!

So, we had to deal with a god with his huge army? There was no hope. Everything was gone before it even started. Hadn't anyone else but me noticed that?

But he seemed to have sensed me. He menacingly pointed the tip of his sword at me.

I decided not to tell anyone what I saw. I didn't want to spread panic or dent our men's morale. It would be such a pity to put an end to all this bravery, magnanimity and self-abnegation. They deserved to meet a glorious and dignified end!!!

"Now!" I yelled with all my might, while feeling that the LightBringer was baying for blood. The horsemen gained momentum and changed the enemy whose first reaction was that of mirth.

Upon seeing how brave and determined our men were, however, as they marched against them at a steady pace, they were taken by storm. They hadn't expected it. They were nonplussed, seeing that such a small army attacked first.

Our horsemen broke through the forefront in the middle. The foot soldiers and I were truing to cover the horsemen sideways.

What I had expected happened. The enemy came behind us, trying to surround us. Then, our archers took over, pummelling whoever was behind us. The clangour of weapons and the hissing sound of the arrows rent the air.

All you could hear were howls and the thud of soulless corpses hitting the ground.

Kron-Ammoth's idea to put copper on the weapons was working just fine. It seemed that these creatures were sensitive to copper.

Everything went to plan. Yet, the enemy troops were endless, outnumbering us. The end wouldn't take long to come...

"I guess you need my help," I heard a familiar voice in my head. "Sorry I'm late. I had to gather as many as I could." I turned around to see where this voice was coming from, but I saw nothing.

"I'm here. Look up," the voice was heard again.

I then raised my eyes to the sky to see a snow-white unicorn flying towards me. It was Leukarat.

"Hop on me," she said as soon as she landed next to me.

"I doubt whether I've ever felt happier to see someone," I noted.

"I'm sure," I heard her voice laugh inside my head.

Our men took heart when the magic creatures arrived. The enemy was surprised once again. Leukarat and I led the way and we marched on towards the enemy.

"We had to come," I heard the voice in my head again. "It's not only you whose existence depends on this battle; ours depends too."

The magic creatures accompanying Leukarat threw themselves into battle. For an instant, everything seemed to be running smoothly. It seemed so strange and beautiful to me watching all these people and magic creatures fight, like nothing had ever driven a wedge between them.

A deafening sound coming from the enemy's buccina rent the air, which showed they were regrouping before they retaliated. There were seemingly millions of them. We wouldn't hold out for much longer.

I saw their chief galloping towards me. So was I. Our swords were raised high. When we neared each other, we crossed them.

I felt myself hit the ground, my LightBringer smashing into pieces. My whole body was in pain from the fall. All my thoughts stalled. That was the end...

I couldn't believe what was going on. How could the LightBringer fall apart so easily? Had everything come to naught, after all? I began to feel that everything became a blur inside of me, while images popped up in my mind...

I could see images of a beautiful emerald green world. I saw the three suns and the seven moons again, then a bright blue light.

They say that this is the kind of images someone gets to see when their end is near. Yet, these images looked so familiar to me. I felt so serene, so I surrendered...

Suddenly, I heard a baby's laughter. With as much strength as I had left, I half-opened my eyes. I saw a female figure holding something in her hands. She seemed to be speaking to someone in front her, but this 'someone' didn't exist. What she held in her hands emitted a bright light.

Her gaze showed she was waiting expectantly for someone to come from afar. All of a sudden, she turned in my direction and we locked gaze. Could she see me? Was it me she was smiling at?

She's Maira. The woman I saw in the desert and in the mirror room!!! She's holding a winged baby that is radiant!!! It's moving its hands and legs. It's laughing its heart out. I feel like she's trying to give me strength, while her face...

This magic face with the beautiful eyes that make me want to get lost in them. This smile of hers that I feel like balm ready to heal all wounds, her name meaning Dream...Why does all this seem so familiar to me?

"Be careful," I suddenly heard Leukarat's voice in my head. "It's magic. They're trying to fool your mind."

I jumped up with all my might. I saw I was on top of Leukarat. The LightBringer was intact. None of this had happened.

Ever since the battle began, the LightBringer had shone and claimed the life of every single enemy in front of me. But they were endless. We wouldn't hold out for much longer. The end loomed ahead again...

Suddenly, some loud and intermittent sounds came from the sky. At first, it sounded like hail, but I realised it was ice. Tips made of ice that fell on the opposite camp.

There were countless of these tips. Like an invisible troop of archers that came out of nowhere to charge our enemies.

Our men and I stopped short in surprise. We ended up gaping at this strange spectacle that cost thousands of lives. One by one, our enemies slumped to the ground. Their numbers dwindled.

Then, a buccina rent the air and the enemy beat a hasty retreat. When they realised what was going on, our men couldn't stop cheering.

"Our task is over. We have to go. See you soon," I heard Leukarat's voice in my head again. "All your deeds during your course in life in this world do not benefit only humans, but also the magic creatures residing in this world. We'll never forget that," she added and disappeared along with the rest of the magic creatures.

I turned to look at our men, who were looking at the peak of the nearest hill. At first, I saw a shine. The longer I looked at it, the more clearly I could make out a female figure with long snow-white hair and a shiny white garment. After a while, this silhouette vanished into thin air.

"The Queen of Ice, the Queen of Snow!" I heard exclamations of admiration around me.

"Who's the Queen of Snow?" I asked whoever happened to be near me.

I've heard so many wondrous things about her and her powers. I've learnt that she's a beautiful and powerful witch. Some people told me that she's said to have answers to everything.

I've also found out that she lives in a grandiose Palace in the North, where everything is made of ice. Whoever enters her Palace can hardly keep their eyes open as everything shines.

It is heard that in her throne room is a huge portrait. It's so beautiful and alive that some believe it's spellbound and the extension of her soul.

Rumour has it that this Queen cloistered herself in there because her heart turned to ice due to a lost love. Yet, nobody knew any more details as to what had happened. Only that the loss of this love made her seer clear of humans.

After the first shock, we cheered and hugged one another, rejoicing in that unexpected and glorious victory in the name of humans.

19

When the news of the triumph spread, a huge feast was held across Len-Bion. Everyone, men and women, young and old, joined in. I could see all those people celebrating, their faces lighting up with joy and gratitude.

I didn't participate, but I liked watching all those happy faces.

Just as our army came back to Len-Bion, people waited to cheer them on as they entered the village. They rhythmically called out my name. The truth is, I got extremely self-conscious. Never before had I received so much adulation in this world.

I sometimes burst into laughter. I saw some young people who had taken part in the battle brag of their achievements to young girls, who would let out some exclamations of fear upon hearing their descriptions. Then, the men held them in their arms reassuringly.

But, above all, I laughed at two friends. They had drunk a lot and were three sheets to the wind. They vied with each other over who had killed the most enemies. They were shouting over which one was the braver of the two.

In their drunken stupor, they seized hold of their guns and, staggering, they headed outside the village, searching for more enemies, so as to prove their bravado.

At some point, Kron-Ammoth came to sit next to me. His eyes looked stern.

"It's time for me to complete what I was telling you about before we get interrupted," he said in a serious tone. "This wall separates the eastern from the western areas of Len-Bion. We are on the eastern side. The destruction you see all around pales before what's threatening the western side."

Kron-Ammoth's words triggered a weird reaction inside of me.

"I don't understand you," I said in puzzlement.

"This huge gate you see is locked," Kron-Ammoth continued. "It once led to the road that connected the eastern and western areas. For quite some time now, our tracers have been telling us about a dark threat hovering in the air. There were so many cries of despair coming from those who tried to warn us. The fact that we ignored all this was our second fatal mistake. As you already know, though, we had other problems to deal with. When we realised the real extent of the danger, it was already too late. An unknown kind of a supreme dark magic came from the west, like a parallel world that appeared out of nowhere, gradually gnawing at ours. This world, like a veil of evil in the form of a new order that brings a new era, spreads like the plague, devouring everything in its path."

"What is new must be welcome only when it's better than the old," I unconsciously thought. "Otherwise, why should there be anything new?"

The old man carried on:

"All the western areas of Len-Bion are now desolate. People left their homes and property. We are the ones left behind. We can't contend with this evil as we know nothing about it. We locked and bolted this gate too, so as to bide time. We cast it in copper. Sooner or later, this threat will knock our door and then it's not only our existence that will be in danger, but our whole world..."

Speechless, I heard the old man's scary words, while at the same time remembering those of Shivi-La regarding what would happen if Betrayal dominated.

So, Betrayal is a dark magic and starts here, Len-Bion...

"You heard what you had to hear. The rest may depend on you...," the old man concluded.

When I was left alone after my conversation with the old man, I thought hard for hours, which seemed like an eternity to me. However, while all these hours were not enough for me to make up my mind, a single moment proved ample time to lead me to an impulse just like this right now.

It seems there are times when a moment, no matter how petty, is stronger than eternity itself...

Maybe it was the feeling I get every time I come across a gate. The feeling that behind a gate hides whatever I seek: redemption, answers and, mainly, you. I'm absolutely certain that you exist...

Maybe it was the fact that I changed my mind about humans. I guess I was way too harsh on them. They actually need help and another chance.

Maybe I simply felt it was my duty as my destiny led me here. One should stoically accept one's destiny.

Maybe it was all this together. The fact that I followed this great impulse. Even now, at the last moment, try as I might, I can't find an answer inside of me as to why I did it.

I asked Kron-Ammoth to get out. I would walk through this threat. I would wend my way into this new dark world that sought to poison the current one. I would acquaint myself with this unknown magic that, taking the form of an epidemic, was about to contaminate everything.

I wanted to walk through it and find out if there was a way I could deal with it.

When Kron-Ammoth told me about all this, he didn't expect me to make such a decision. Despite his initial misgivings, my persistence proved stronger. I made for the wall. I reached the gate. Once the gate closed behind me, I'd be left alone.

There were some people, including Shira-Tuth, who asked to join me. I refused flat-out. I couldn't put them in such a danger.

While I wasn't a human, I stood more chances of achieving something. I had to do it on my own. Once again, these men's bravery had touched me.

Shira-Tuth pleaded with me to accept his bow. At first, I refused to accept such a gift. I knew what it meant to him. But he showed how much he believed in me. He said he would wait for me to come back. He was sure I would return. I couldn't say no to such a polite gesture.

But there was something else. Kron-Ammoth thought of using an age-old spell. It was risky as he would use it for the first time. However, it was the last thing he could do to protect Len-Bion.

With this spell, Len-Bion, at least what was left of it in the eastern areas, would be covered in an invisible veil. Only the eyes of the soul would be able to see it.

I had already used these eyes once. I peeked inside my soul, so I stood a chance of going back.

I reach the gate. I take one last look behind me. I felt weird seeing all those silent people eyeing me agonisingly, like they doubted I would make it...

I moved on, hearing the sound of the gate as it shut behind me. In a while, all alone, with the LightBringer as my only companion, I would be in the bowels of this threat.

It was a threat that lurked and spread silently, waiting for a chance to wipe out everything in its path.

20

I found myself inside tis dark world. I could never imagine what I saw: a black rocky lunar landscape without a trace of life.

The wind was hissing a menacing melody. Overhead stretched a gloomy grey wintry sky. I carried on for quite some time until I saw some unfamiliar and weird creatures.

These creatures looked much akin to humans. They didn't seem to be human. They were wandering around as if hypnotised.

I didn't feel there was any soul inside their bodies. How could there be? Who could have ever created such a thing?

I felt nothing. Everything seemed to be nothing. How could someone deal with nothing? One can confront one's enemies with a sword's blade.

One can also face monsters. What could a sword, even a LightBringer, do to confront nothingness?

I looked around searching for a sign that could lead me somewhere, but in vain. It was monotonous scenery, the same dead landscape...

Some weird thoughts were reeling in my mind. I remembered some old human stories. I don't know why. These stories spoke of Love, Faith, Devotion, Joy, Hope and Happiness.

Those were beautiful Nymphs that were dancing insouciantly. Humans named after them emotions and values that embellished and gave meaning to their life. Of course, I never met them.

Do they still exist? Why did they disappear? Perhaps they sensed all this was coming. Are they hiding in the bowels of the earth, waiting for this storm to blow over?

What became of Angels? Humans often spoke of them and how they protected them in difficult times.

I can't sense any trace of demons or monsters. I feel no such presence.

It seems that nobody and nothing can stop this parallel world from spreading as, taking the form of a new era, it contaminates everything like an incurable virus.

These thoughts are so strange as they unconsciously visit my mind. Nothing here works according to the reality I knew. The same holds for my thoughts.

Throughout my course, I carefully examined these creatures. With the passage of time, I realised these creatures lost their souls on their own.

At some point, I was horrified to see treat their own bodies so profanely. It was something I couldn't explain...

I remembered the Golem again. That anthropoid that was the product of magic made of stone and clay. It had no soul, but at least respected its body. It tried to give it beauty in any way it could...

What I've always firmly believed is that every body is a small temple, something sacred. However, instead of small temples, I saw buildings full of excrement. Why do they do this? Why do they molest their own bodies and souls?

They look like human creatures; maybe they are. What is it that transmuted them?

I plodded on. Later, much to my surprise, I met similar creatures which I felt had a breath of soul. They seemed to recognise something in me. They approached me as if in supplication. No voice came out of their mouths.

I walked past them. I covered my face with my mantle and quickened my gait. My identity must not be revealed.

What mattered the most was my mission. But in vain. These other creatures had no soul, so they figured out. Some of them charged me menacingly.

I grabbed hold of my LightBringer handle. It started shimmering. At the sight of it, these creatures took to their heels in fright.

I had the first information that could help in my task. They were scared of light...

Some of these creatures attacked and mocked those that came up to me in supplication.

So, I had a second piece of information: Can nothingness give place to mockery? I wondered if bravery, honour and pride can face mockery...

A hissing sound was heard coming from a spear that rent the air. I felt unbearable pain. An arrow lodged in my back, then another one and another one...

I pressed my lips in an expression of rage and indignation.

Weren't these creatures able to face their enemy head-on? Even demons and monsters did that out of respect. Had these creatures stooped so low?

I've always respected my enemy. I honoured him by facing him head-on. The enemy is an honourable and respectable person. He has the courage and dignity to face you with honesty, to show you he's against you.

For someone to face their enemy, they have to get better and progress. Therefore, the enemy is useful as he forces us to become better...

At some point, the pain got me down. All strength oozed out of my body. I lost balance. I would have slumped to the ground if I hadn't leant on my sword handle.

The only thought that got stuck in my head was that I had to stand ramrod straight. I wouldn't give them the pleasure of seeing me fall. Nor would I honour them by facing them.

In a fit of indignation and pride, I carried on, while ignoring everything. I was so appalled by those creatures that the only thing I must do was turn my back on them.

After a while, I walked away. Then, they stopped attacking me. With the passage of time, I came to realise that these arrows weren't lethal but poisonous.

Would I become one of those creatures myself? I shuddered at the very thought. I felt desperate...

Then, a new power took hold of me. Maybe it was that 'something' which protected me. That 'something' which resides inside of me and heals everything!!!

I have a wedge of light inside of me. Maybe with this I'd heal myself. Maybe I just needed some time.

For as long as the poison ran through my veins, I wouldn't be able to go back. Those waiting for me ran the risk of getting contaminated as well. I couldn't take this risk.

Apart from that, this poison keeps the eyes of the soul from opening. For as long as I carried it inside of me, I would never find my way back.

That's what I was thinking when I saw a hill in front of me. I decided to get there. Maybe it was the right place, I thought to myself...

When I reached its lonely peak, I looked around. It was the same monotonous dead landscape. I stuck my sword in the ground and sat on the rock silently.

I'd stay there for as long as was necessary, until that poison was gone. Time would tell if my reasoning was sound or not.

Suddenly, the LightBringer began to shine again. Perhaps that was the sign I had been looking for. I had a brainwave. If it proved right, then there was a way, after all.

The LightBringer kept shining, lodged as it was in the ground. I thought it could attract those creatures that carried a breath of soul within and weren't afraid of the light.

I had to wait until my wounds healed and see if these creatures would gather around me. I would be able to breathe a new life into them. I would open the eyes of their soul as much as I could.

Yes, I would fight and face the enemy the way he did. I'd be the one who would contaminate him. I would serve as an antidote. I would become a contaminant among so many others.

That was the hardest situation I'd ever been in...

I kept mulling over the words the three mysterious women had once told me in the cave of the Ancient Ones: 'You have to remember you're a warrior. Don't you ever forget it'. That was what the mischievous spirit also told me.

A warrior must use his brains as well as his sword blade. I had learnt that lesson very well. Of course, the circumstances under which I lived had also played a role...

I have no choice right now. I'll meet a glorious end in the battlefield, as I think befits me, or I'll wipe out this plague once and for all.

I was lost in thought while sitting at the lonely peak. My loneliness was once again my only company during those hard moments.

I had wronged my loneliness, taking it for a nightmare, but in fact it was my friend and companion that always reached out her hand to me.

I heard some voices in my head.

I recalled those words that told me that, if I listened out carefully, I would hear my soul speak to me. I would hear her speak in a little boy's voice.

At first, it would speak in a hushed tone. As I listened to it carefully, this voice would grow louder.

Of course, there are other voices as well. Seductive voices like those of the Sirens.

With false hopes, they promise happiness through illusions. Their only concern, though, is for us not to hear the voice of the soul. They want to lead us to disaster.

We have to resist these voices and try to hear what the soul has to tell us. We must make this voice grow louder, so as to deaden the voices of the Sirens.

Is this why these creatures lost their souls? Did they ignore its voice until it petered out? If this voice is lost, how will someone talk to themselves?

My thoughts were interrupted by some screams coming from a distance. I was so engrossed that I lost track of space around the hill.

I stood up. I saw countless of these creatures charge me menacingly. Unfortunately, though, I attracted the wrong creatures.

I felt their fear of light. However, it was this fear that urged them to attack me. They were closing in. I braced myself for battle.

The LightBringer in my hands started to shake. I felt it had such a will as to attack an enemy. They should understand that they are no longer a problem to me, but I am their problem.

I let out a scream and charged them. They were caught unawares. They hadn't expected it. They were falling on me all the time. My sword was so fierce that I couldn't stop it. There were countless of them...

I pretended to be chasing them, so as to make them draw back. Then, I went back to the top of the hill to bide time and rest. This happened again and again, but it was futile. Ho much longer would I hold out?

At some point, these creatures realised I was tired. They came closer to the foot of the hill, but stopped there.

We exchanged looks for quite some time, but neither side made any move. Then, I began to feel their mockery.

I was overcome with rage. This rage clouded my pride. My thoughts were no longer clear.

They wanted to disorient me, so that I would lose self-control. I'd be an easy victim. The poison was to blame for all this that I still had inside.

I had got rid of most of it, so I wasn't in danger. I could feel it. Still, this little amount of poison inside harmed me. It was my weak point. I realised that, while I reacted, their poison did me more harm and that's exactly what they wanted.

I suddenly felt a new strength running through my veins. I heard the voice of my soul that was like a little child...

"What am I doing?" I wondered. "These creatures can't harm me if I don't let them harm me. They take advantage of my own power against myself. Nothing exists unless I give it substance!!!"

I was laughing out loud. They looked so pathetic to me. The more I looked at them, the louder my laughter grew.

I made fun of them with all sorts of grimaces.

"You can't do anything to me," I shouted.

I caught myself acting like a child. I don't remember ever feeling like that before. I was having such a great time. It was such an unprecedented feeling for me during those strange moments...

The creatures started falling to the ground. They were keeping their ears shut. They were writhing, as if they were in pain. That was my first blow against them.

I discovered in awe that the third and most serious clue against them was revealed to me. Nothingness and mockery make the poison stronger. A child's heart and soul, however, dissolve it.

Here's the antidote. All we have to do is become and remain little children. There are no dirty actions, but dirty thoughts. A little child, naive and innocent as it is, can't be characterised as dirty.

The child's purity acts like a fire of purification. While you keep this childhood fire alive, you have nothing to fear. I can go back to Len-Bion.

Len-Bion is the last shelter for humans. Anyone can go there. Childhood will banish all traces of the poison. It will open the eyes of the soul.

I won such a difficult battle without the blade of a single sword. The LightBringer seemed to chafe at this. I could barely prove I was its rightful owner...

21

I went back. Besides, I learnt what I needed. Deep down, I never stopped wondering what it was that triggered everything. It was the last and probably the most important thing I had to find out. Since I was going back to Len-Bion, I would have all the time in the world to explore it.

I wandered around for a few days, yet no sign of the gate that would lead me back. I began to worry. I was afraid that the poison that remained inside of me was behind it. But why? I had found the antidote.

Maybe I had to do something. Was it possible that I might now find my way back? I was gripped by a sense of despair.

While I was wandering around in the bowels of this unfamiliar threat, inside the swaddling clothes of Betrayal, I felt like the hours, days and time in general amounted to nothing. But Time didn't show any signs of existence in this place, anyway.

Is its absence a kind of punishment? What is this oft-quoted phrase 'the time is ripe'? Punishment or redemption? Am I on the right track? Was I led here in a futile roaming? Maybe I was trapped in a kind of timeless prison?

From the bottom of my heart, I hope nothing of the sort is true. It would be tragic to end up from the world of humans, which I deemed to be my prison, into an infinitely worse jail. Especially now that I began to view humans and their world from a different perspective...

The thoughts of all those who pinned their hopes on me made me feel somewhat better. I realised the gravity of my responsibility and importance of my mission.

The result wouldn't only have an impact on the people of Len-Bion; it would also affect their whole kind, their world, the remaining ones as well as posterity.

It would also affect my own wandering. I had to prove my mettle, I had to make it. I was nearing the end, I could feel it...

These thoughts got stuck in my mind. For a moment, I stopped short. I clenched my fist and carried on with determination.

At some point, I saw smoke on the horizon. My hopes were rekindled. Nothing was over yet. My instinct was telling me what it was the last direction I had to follow.

As I got closer, I could see some huge black rocks standing before me. Among them was a road. All I had to do was find out what was at its end...

I gingerly made my way. I was walking on the left, trying to hide behind the rocks. There was no sign of life or any other activity. Still, I had to brace myself for everything.

At the end of the road loomed a huge house made from the same black rock.

Roughly hewn rocks in strange formations that made up an uncanny jarring whole. Who could possibly have created this huge monstrosity? It must have been a temple or a shrine.

I went closer. These huge boulders formed a natural circle. This strange building was in the middle. It looked like the crater of a volcano.

On the walls of the rocks were some evenly spaced out entrances. They were small mouths of caves with anaglyphs. I wondered where they could possibly lead — probably to some dark corner of the Abyss. I was sure all the answers I sought lay in here.

I suddenly saw in the distance a human figure enter one of those mouths. I was surprised to realise that it was a Mahakwe. I remembered the descriptions I had heard of them. Besides, their black habit was quite distinctive.

The priests of Aramos were behind it all. This couldn't even cross my mind. The mystery slowly began to unravel, but the narrations I heard were all true.

I cautiously neared the building perched on the cluster of rocks, so as not to be seen. I had to find a way to get in. All my senses were alert. I knew the Mahakwe were dangerous opponents.

I carefully looked in all directions. No one else seemed to be around. I unsheathed my LightBringer and made for the middle of the crater.

I was in the heart of this nightmare. There was something in the air that made me feel weird. I felt the terror and the threat lurking in every corner...

At some point, the LightBringer began to tremble. I felt its wish to fight. I looked right. There was a Mahakwe around, who sensed my presence.

I wasted no time. The LightBringer couldn't be restrained. Its blade gave off some weird shines. Its thirst for battle was insatiable. Within seconds, Mahakwe was dead and it was a matter of time before the rest of them sensed my presence.

I ran towards the entrance of the temple. This entrance was the shape of an arch. It was made of bricks. As I crossed the gate, I stormed in the corridor with such momentum that those who saw me were left nonplussed.

Some of them lunged forward to stop me. Fortunately, I was the one endowed with the privilege of surprise until they realised what happened.

In a flash, another two Mahakwe fell on my sword. At the same time, by means of heavy blows and thanks to my knees, I knocked out whoever stood in my way. The Mahakwe were rooted to the spot, seeing that they were unable to stop me.

When they regained composure, their voices spread all over the place: "A profane trespasser! Stop him! Down with him!"

I carried on with the same aplomb. I didn't look back. Still, I didn't even know where to head. I had no specific destination to follow. I decided to cross the corridor all the way to its end.

At some point, I realised that I was going downhill, thinking that this corridor was endless. The Mahakwe were running after me.

The lower I got, the hotter I felt. This meant I was moving towards the heart of the volcano.

In the distance, I saw a small door, which was open. The closer I got, the clearer I made out some steps. When I walked in, I descended the stairs at the same pace.

When they reached the door, the Mahakwe stopped chasing me. Like there was something in there they wouldn't dare confront.

I heard someone say behind me: "He's a lunatic for sure. He's going straight into Aramos's residence."

"Let him be. There's no turning back," someone else added. "He decided on his own end."

I stopped short. I wanted to make sure that no one was after me. I took no heed of their words. I was sure they simply did it to intimidate me.

I carried on going down those stairs — at a much slower pace this time. In a while, my tortuous descent took me to another door.

I crossed it and ended up in a big enclosed space. I couldn't characterise it as a room or as a hall.

Its walls were the volcano itself. There were a series of gigantic columns in perfect arrangement.

"What a weird place," I whispered, while the heat in there was unbearable…

22

I had no option but to carry on. At the same time, I was scanning the place. I plodded on slowly and carefully, so as to be able to parry any blow.

Suddenly, the ground began to shake. I took a step back. A few yards in front of me was a ring of fire. Through this fiery ring came out a thick puff of smoke. I could also hear some weird voices. I couldn't catch what they were saying.

A while later, some otherworldly bolts of lightning spread all over the place, while thousands of cries rent the air, just like an army attacking the enemy.

I clutched my sword, so as to be alert. I didn't mean to take to my heels. Strangely enough, I felt nothing across the handle — neither wish for battle nor any aversion to it. Never before had the LightBringer acted like that...

After a while, the fire was gone in the same mysterious way. The voices ceased. As the smoke dissipated, an imposing figure hove into view. I realised pretty soon... "Aramos," I let out a whisper.

The puff of smoke dissolved. Before me stood the grandiose god Aramos, whose name struck terror into people's hearts. He was twice as tall as I was and clad in a shiny pitch-black suit of armour.

I marvelled at its decoration. It had such beautiful engravings.

His huge sword as just as impressive. Its blade was made from black metal and its handle featured an engraved cut-out of a dragon's foot. His face wasn't visible as it was covered in his helmet that was decorated with bat's wings.

I stood in awe and surprise. It was the figure I saw in a vision as the chief of the enemies during the Ankhammon Battle, the same form depicted by the statues in Len-Bion. So, it was here that the Mahakwe had tried to play with my mind...

"Who dares storm into my home, shaking my silence?" his imposing voice was heard.

My mind was overcome with rage.

"The one who will put an end to the plans schemed by you and your priests," I replied. "I don't know what you've done to other worlds, but I won't let you destroy this one. I wonder how a god can be so heartless and ruthless, ready to destroy."

"So, you've come over to face me, eh?" he said, cracking a thunderous and sarcastic laugh through his helmet, which reverberated throughout the hall.

"Keep this laugh to yourself," I shouted. "Brace yourself now, for you will meet the same end as your priests."

It was weird that I felt no reaction on the part of the LightBringer. Still, I didn't mean to back down. I charged him, letting out a war cry.

Aramos was unflappable, waiting for my blow. At the right time, he parried it with great force. When the two blades crossed, a loud clangour was heard and a light dazzled me.

Aramos's blow was so heavy that I was hurled in the air. I hit the wall, then landed on the ground, my LightBringer hovering in midair.

Anyone else wouldn't have stood such a blow. The LightBringer protected me. In vain. Everything showed that I earned a few seconds of life.

I was in so much pain after the blow that I was unable to move. I couldn't react. Aramos headed towards me silently. The clangour of his armour rent the air. Every step he took was a countdown for me.

He raised his sword, holding its handle in both hands. He intended to wipe me out. That was not part of a vision. It was a real fact...

Was that my end? Was it the deathblow I had longed for in the past? I didn't mind, though. I'd have another chance to seek another life in another world.

Maybe that was part of destiny. All this probably happened for me to come to this point. So be it. I accept it without much ado if this destiny is to bring me closer to you.

I turned my gaze upon Aramos. "What are you waiting for? Do what you have to do. The human world will be destroyed. I'm trapped in an infinitely more nightmarish prison. On my end, I did what I had to do with bravery and honour. Do the same. Give me the end that will grant me Redemption," I said with as much strength as I had left.

Upon hearing these words, Aramos stopped short and put his sword down. He silently stood over me for quite some time.

"You're not human," he said as he sized me up. "Now I know who you are, but I find it so strange to see you, of all people, defend humans. Tell me, what is the real reason why you came here? Have you come here for humans' sake or yourself? Have you come here to find closure or destroy yourself? Not even you know it, right?"

I had no strength to answer. I simply nodded my head, writhing in pain.

"Humans," continued Aramos, "are the strangest beings in the world. They're destructible and weak, but they're endowed with tenacity, which makes them so strong. Ever since they were created, they have been striving to find food every single day, to mate, to pursue all sorts of goals, even to recognise their emotions. But this is their choice, not a dictate of nature. They even try to tame nature itself. If they see fit, they're capable of contradicting anyone, just like you are doing now. I don't know if you've realised that, but you're so much like them. Of course, you would never fall victim to vanity, like they do, nor would you ever surrender to insipid passions. It is them who weave a net around themselves. Time may not be beneficial for each and every one of them, but it is favourable to them as a species. But time cannot be tamed, no matter how hard they try to attend to their legacy. The spectre of death is constantly hanging over their heads. Some think this is the end, while others are terrified at the very thought of it as they do not know. Their passage to life is so short, like a summer cloud, which is soon blown away. What they know is so scant, even what concerns their own existence. What will I call them? How can such conflicting things reside inside a single being? They fight for their freedom, but they oppress themselves with obsessions and traps inside their minds. They pursue happiness, yet they are rooted to the spot when they see a door leading to it close. At the same time, they turn a blind eye to so many other doors that are wide open in front of them beckoning to them. For centuries, I've been feeling their horror when they refer to my name. I see their scared faces when they enter my temples. They believe I am responsible for many things. They attribute it all to me. They think I am a god of evil. Why? I often found their naïveté such fun, but there were times when I thought it was sorrowful. They try to explain notions unfamiliar to them through their weaknesses and ignorance. They are capable of killing for that. Do you know how many crimes humans have made, preying on gods' name? That's what humans are like, that's what those you came here to defend are like. They justify their illegal actions, claiming that each god is like a father. But tell me, what kind of father would ever need to be worshipped like that? What father would like to keep the truth from his children? What father would like to see his own children getting killed? What father wouldn't want to see his descendants grow up with love, wisdom, prudence and virtue? What father wouldn't want his children to prosper and create, thus growing his inheritance even more? Is there a father who will hear his child shout 'Water, mum' and not offer it to him, just because she didn't hear him and he didn't say 'father'? The same holds for every mother. So, I'm the god of evil...Does any human know what evil is really like, so as to pay me back? I am the night that succeeds the day. The end that complements the beginning. The darkness that surrounds the light. What's wrong with that? This is my role, after all. I am a god and there are many more like me. Many a time, when I saw humans pray, I wondered who they really address. Do they know we have nothing to do with the Creator of All Things? Do they know that we too are creations of this Supreme Being? We too were made for a purpose. Through our position, we have undertake the role assigned to us. The same is true of every creature, regardless of whether some of them, like humans, do not know it. Even you and me: we can't escape our destiny. At the same time, we are obliged to guard whatever we have been commanded to do. Do you understand what I'm saying?"

I was listening to him in a daze.

"Humans need a second chance," I whispered with as much strength as I had left.

"That's true," replied Aramos. "I have to restore some things. Everyone must know that I have nothing to do with the actions of the Mahakwe. They used my name to justify their deeds. I simply waited to see how humans would react and they sent for you. So be it...All the prayers and entreaties are not enough. Whoever is unable to help themselves cannot accept any help. Stand up and come closer. Don't be afraid."

Suddenly, I could feel no pain in my body. I stood up and hesitantly made in his direction.

"I followed your journey. All the things you discovered inside are so wondrous! Everyone had better follow the same route."

Upon saying this, Aramos raised his palm. Then, a black leather-bound book appeared. It looked very old. I wondered what it could contain.

"The pages of this book are blank," he said. "They're waiting for you to fill them. Write here everything concerning your wandering. Since you decided to defend humans and believe that they deserve a second chance, let your words become a message and precious legacy. Will you do it?"

I forced a smile. I couldn't believe what was happening. I would be an angel, a messenger, that would deliver the message. A fallen angel, but an angel nonetheless.

"I'll do it," I replied.

"Always look at the journey, not the destination," he continued. "Consider the route your reward. As for the rest, let your destiny guide you. When the time comes, you'll find what you seek."

Aramos raised his head again. A black puff of smoke enveloped me. I felt the earth shake under my feet.

While I was being engulfed by this cloud, I heard his last words: "The Mahakwe didn't tarnish only my name. Because of their sacrilege, they also defiled my house. I'll make sure their creation becomes their prison."

His voice petered out. When the smoke began to dissipate, I couldn't believe my eyes. Everything around me disappeared. I was standing before the gate of Len-Bion...

23

It was over, at last! Perhaps no one had expected me to make it.

When I reach the top of the hill ahead of me, my eyes will see Len-Bion again. It looks so beautiful in springtime sun. I've never seen it from up here in broad daylight.

I can see the blue waters of the ocean stroking its shores. I turn my gaze back. I see the mountains towering around me. From there start the rivers like sources, only to disappear into the sea's embrace later on.

Far afield, I can see the rolling meadows and the thick forests pulsating with life and vegetation.

They're right, those who call it 'The Land of Life'!

I wondered what would happen if I had lost. But now that everything's changed, it's the best opportunity for humans to reconcile with the magic creatures.

My eyes fell on Len-Bion's huge gate that was open yet again.

From where I stand, humans look as tiny as ants wandering around. They are working laboriously. It's a matter of time before they build their place from scratch.

I remember joy on their surprised faces the moment they saw me back. I felt strange seeing them cheer me on and show me so much love. They considered me something important.

I remember Shira-Tuth, who couldn't stop hugging me and shouting he believed in me. I had kept my promise to him. I came back to give him his bow.

The people of Len-Bion asked me to stay with them. I'd love to. For the first time, I felt I belonged somewhere. But not now.

I refused. I might come back when my wandering was over. My first priority will always be to find the answers I seek.

I turned my eyes where I could see a different aspect of Len-Bion. Behind the mountaintops where a totally different world sprawled, a world of trap and death.

A vast desert and endless marshes from which so many had never escaped.

This place always knew how to keep a strange balance. It knew how to hide its secrets. Humans themselves had to learn that. They had to learn how to keep their balance...

Len-Bion had fallen prey to human avarice and vanity in the past. The recent danger was a plan called Betrayal and it could prove lethal.

Humans had just been spared the worst nightmare — a nightmare that, like the black waters of the Ocean, was about to smother their existence.

After that adventure, nothing will be the same for me, this world, or humans. I only hope what changed will make us all better, so that we can become more optimistic for the future.

No one can imagine what powers it may hide. Not even a human can imagine that, although he is superior to the other creatures of this world.

Everyone hides an unexplored world within. They will be amazed to find out how many things they can discover about themselves.

There's also the enigmatic appearance of the Queen of Snow. It was sudden and determined the outcome of the battle.

What was it that made him turn up out of nowhere? Will she fight on our side? Why did she disappear so suddenly after the end of the battle?

Her presence was discussed much more than the battle itself and the victory we achieved thanks to it.

My eyes fell on the big book Aramos gave me. I will do it. I'm going to write in it my wanderings as legacy for humans.

After all, Len-Bion is a symbol. It's the place where Betrayal was born. It's the place where humans begin to get reborn.

There are surely leftovers of Betrayal scattered throughout the place. With determination, it's only a matter of time before they get wiped out. I will fight them wherever I come across them.

I'm sure humans, for many generations to go, will still remember and sing of Len-Bion until it's left in their memory like a dream that may never have existed...

These were my thoughts, while I was in my favourite place — on top of a hill, feeling the wind pierce through me...

There are times when I have the need to feel the Wind. Its outburst feed the Fire inside of me. It makes me feel much stronger.

Inside my head, memories are still running. The intense feelings from the battle are still raging and flowing within. Never before had I lived something so intense.

I have to find the Queen of Snow, to tall to her. She provides answers to everything!!!

I take a deep breath. I look at the vast void. A veil of fog is stroking the wet soil. The smell of fresh grass wafts in the air...

"Are you ready? We have a long way to go," I heard the voice in my mind that interrupted my thoughts.

"Yes, I'm ready," I replied.

It was my favourite friend Leukarat. She offered once again to help me. She knew where the palace of the Queen of Snow was. You could go there only by flying.

I hopped on her back. After a while, we were heading north. Flying is such a familiar feeling. I'd give my all to grow wings...

Countless hours went by. I was overwhelmed with thoughts while we were flying.

I was curious to see how the LightBringer and the wedge of Light inside of me would react to the frozen heart of the Queen of Snow...

I realised that, for the first time, thanks to my friend, I wouldn't need to look for or follow tracks.

Tracks...

Everyone in this world seeks and follows tracks. Still, how many of them follow the tracks of their soul?

"We're getting close," I heard Leukarat's voice in my head once again, which interrupted my thoughts.

I was sure she could hear everything all the time. It's just that she was polite enough not to intervene in my thoughts. She's a wonderful creature...

I already felt the icy-cold wind whipping my face with chunks of snow.

After a while, before us sprawled the Queen's palace that was sparkling. It was of impeccable beauty, much more impressive than its descriptions.

The ice the palace was made of was crafted with consummate skill. I counted seven tall towers whose tips touched the sky.

Leukarat stopped in front of the palace gate. It was just as impressive and decorated with reliefs.

What hand or magic had created something so wondrous?

"I'll be waiting for you here," I heard Leukarat's voice inside my head.

I nodded and walked towards the gate. I was ready to meet the Queen of Snow...

I entered the palace. A cursory glance was enough for me to ascertain that it was just as impressive on the inside. Everything sparkled, as I used to hear others' narratives.

I saw the throne in the middle of the hall. It was infinitely prettier than rumour had it.

It was made from white gold, studded with colourful stones and chiselled with ornate engravings. It was a perfect match for the shining white ambience around it.

Right above the throne was the portrait of a blonde girl. It can't have been her.

I didn't have the time to scan the place around me. I heard an imposing loud female voice say: "I chose you."

I turned my gaze and saw her standing in the middle of the staircase that led upstairs. She was the Queen of Snow.

Her tiara and sceptre were made of the same material as the throne. They looked equally astounding. They shone with the engravings and the precious gems.

Her long snow-white hair cascaded down her snow-white garment. In her blue eyes shone the grandiose white ambience.

"Why did you choose me?" I asked, admiring her appearance.

"You will lead my frozen army," she replied. "We will spend the Winter all over the world. Only you can lead my army."

"There's no way I'm going to do that..."

"You have no choice," she interrupted me in an imperative tone.

"Try me," I said in a haughty voice.

She raised her sceptre. Countless shards of ice came undone from various spots inside the room. Within seconds, their innumerable sharp tips were hovering in midair, ready to charge me.

I held my LightBringer. It didn't want to fight. That struck me as odd. Still, I had to brace myself for what was to come.

She put her sceptre down. The sharp ends were hurled at me.

I instantly unsheathed my LightBringer, which emitted a strong light. It rippled through the room, a ray hitting the portrait above the throne.

Suddenly, the earth began to shake. Everything around me was moving, about to collapse.

I turned my head towards the Queen. I saw her lying on the floor and ran to her. When I got near, I saw a girl in her place — it was the girl in the portrait.

I bent over her, shaking her body and shouting:

"Why? Why did you attack me?"

In a weak voice, her eyes half-closed, she started recounting a story: "He loved me with all his heart. He did all he could to show that to me. And I was madly in love with him. I don't know what came over me. I don't know what I was thinking and why. My mind was stuck on riches and power. I mocked him, although I loved him. I was always on his case. At some point, I broke his heart and he disappeared. I married a King. I had all I wanted in this life. But it was all futile without him. I missed him so much! One day, I learnt sadness had killed him. I realised I had lost him forever. My heart turned to ice. After a while, my breath too began to freeze until I became what I am now...

"Don't you ever defy your heart and soul. Don't you ever let yourself turn into what I've become..."

But I didn't care about her story. I didn't want to hear anything else. I wanted answers!!! I wanted to know how I was going to find you and go back where I belonged!!!

I kept shaking her weak and still body.

"Why did you do that? Why did you attack me? Tell me!!!"

She tried to open her eyes one last time.

"To pay me back the freedom I've just given you," she said.

I was puzzled. These words rang a bell. Then, I heard a flutter and saw a white dove fly away. How weird!!! It was the dove in the cave of the Ancient Ones.

"Don't worry. What you seek is near" were her last words.

She breathed her last in my arms, then vanished.

I let out a scream of rage and disillusion. Everything around me was tumbling down. I had to leave that place straight away.

I ran out. When I was away, I looked back, only to see an illustrious palace plunging into the icy-cold earth.

I was seized by a huge wave of despair...

So, that's why all this had happened, eh? For the sake of love. What is Love?

Does it have a specific plot? Is it a need? Is it a link on Fate's chain? Was it made for every single person to wear it without any choice?

It's so weird how someone can be overwhelmed with Love and get addicted to it...

Is it Magic, so that someone may be unable to react, surrendering to her allure? Is it Love intended only for humans?

What am I saying? I too experience it, although I'm not human. I know damn well that it can rule a life...

Could it be love what leads to or rules Infinity?

The supreme unexplored destinations.

But tell me...

Would you be scared to look at Infinity with me?

You shouldn't...I'll be by your side.

I'll hold your hand.

Would you be scared to look at Vastness with me?

You shouldn't...I'll be there with you.

I'll hold you tight.

I caught myself laughing my heart out. I remembered the words of the spirit: "Don't start asking the same questions..."

Leukarat watched me silently at first. Then, she tried to console me. She didn't make it.

I asked her to leave. She would drop me off somewhere far away from Len-Bion. I don't like bidding farewell. This puts me in mind of an end, although there's a new beginning in each end.

I prefer to cherish all things beautiful.

The only end I seek is that of my wandering.

I want to find you, so that I can be where I really belong...

24

Not even I remember how much longer I wandered around...

The desert was a time trap. Like a cobweb trapping and gradually devouring someone until they lose consciousness. I reached a place that seemed familiar to me. I'd been there before. I could make out a village on the horizon. Of course...

That's where I must have left that girl who had lost her way a long time ago. So, I was close to the source of the spirits. It's so miraculous and strange that some things come full circle...

There must have been a reason that I was here again.

I was gazing around until I heard a voice addressing me:

"Aiaibamon, why do you keep approaching the humans' residential area? Have you realised you don't belong to their world?"

I turned around to see a young woman.

She continued: "Your world is the world of the Spirits. Only there will your agitated soul find peace, which befits it. Sever your bonds with the world of humans. Don't make your ordeal even worse. You otherworldly tormented creature, aren't you sick and tired of feeling a pariah among them? Aren't you tired of seeing them gather around you? Of having them size you up in order to satisfy their curiosity by fingering your wounds? Can't you hear them whine every day, unable to seize their lives? They beg Fate, Time and Life to satisfy their wishes, unable as they are to face the smallest difficulty. When one of them is granted to them, they throw them away indiscriminately like dishwater, loathing the fact that they were realised. They feel safer in misery. They prefer to complain about unjust fate that is haunting them, while they spurn opportunity whenever it presents itself. They're so insane! What are you doing among them? All the mountains on Earth aren't enough to bridge the gap between you and them. Don't listen to the voices of those who try to convince you that your curse is a blessing. You poor little creature, the one you seek does not exist. Why do you turn a blind eye? She's yet another part of your deception, yet another shroud wrapped around the rotten body of the nightmare that's hounding you. Fates threw you into this soul-destructive Nekyia[1] as they envied you for daring to grow wings without their approval.

You threw off the yokes of your soul. You dared feel free and happy even for a single moment as you're uncompromising. You were sentenced to these very fetters you dared break.

Don't put any more fetters on your worn-out body. Don't let humans approach you, trying to touch your curse and seek illusions. Yes, that's what they want from you: illusions!

There's nothing else you can do for them, since they're unable to do anything for themselves.

They prefer to stick their heads in the sand like an ostrich, inside the illusions of your curse. Woe betide them...

They do not know that everything in life is like a sheet metal. The more you pull it, the more it stretches and strikes back with greater force.

I can't stand seeing you like that, o tamer of pain and sorrow! I know my pain is nothing but a speck of sand compared to yours after your futile wandering.

Accept reality, Aiaibamon. Your wandering is futile!!!

I'm sure you wonder who I am and why I'm saying all this to you. Yes, I'm that little girl you found crying and saying that she lost her way. You helped me and now I want to pay you back.

Back then, I spoke with a little girl's heart and mouth. Now I speak to you with a human's heart and mouth.

Your thoughts are poison!!! Humans aren't ready to accept them. Go back to the world of Spirits. Carry on walking among the shadows.

Only in the Abyss of your Sorrow and the Desert of your Loneliness will you find shelter. Go away, Aiaibamon. I can't stand my heart writhing in pain as I see you..."

---

1   In ancient Greek cult-practice and literature, a *nekyia* or nekya (Ancient Greek: νέκυια ἡ νέκυα) is a "rite by which ghosts were called up and questioned about the future," i.e., necromancy

With her head bowed, the young woman turned on her heels towards the village...

"Wait, Woman!!!" I shouted angrily. "I've been listening to your words all this time as they rang in my ears like vipers' hiss. Before you leave, you'll listen to my words too."

She stopped short, her back still turned to me.

"How dare you tell me that the one I'm searching for does not exist and she's only part of my delusion? How dare you say that without knowing? If you did know, you would know I'm the one who would wish it were a delusion. If this were true, I would at least discover it. Unfortunately, though, it's not a delusion. It's a call, like Spring calls flowers to bloom and they respond. Fooled and lost is the one who ignores this call. Rest assured that I consider this a far worse condemnation. You called my thoughts poison to humans as they do more harm than good. I assure you that I don't give a damn about that. I was the one who decided to help them fight Betrayal and be given an opportunity to make a fresh start. I never urged anyone to come closer to me, nor am I to blame if humans act like nocturnal butterflies. They seek and follow the moonlight. They mistake it for the flame of my soul, that's why they get burnt when they come closer. Am I to blame for their inability to pursue their aspirations? If they're unworthy of realising their goals? If they're afraid to touch their dreams? If they settle for substitutes and illusions? I hope many things change for them now... Let them learn how to pay the price, like I do mine so willingly. This is the only way for someone to find the way to the top...Bear in mind that, if the one I'm looking for exists in this world, she will become one with my fire. She won't get burnt by it. I'm well aware that I belong to the world of Spirits. Yes, I dared grow wings without asking for anyone's permission. But this is an acquisition I earned on my own merit. Maybe the Fates threw me into this abyss out of envy. Maybe they want to test me to make sure that I really deserve to have these wings. For this reason alone, my wandering is not futile. All this pain and sorrow I felt are my spoils, so to speak. No one can take them away from me. You ask me to leave, to go away. Do you mean I have to hide like a scared dog? Would you rather I shed crocodile tears, making others take pity on me for a small consideration? The proud soul of the warrior inside of me would never deign to do such a thing. You think I'm blind, but you seem to ignore how short-sighted you are. You can't discern that the Abyss of Sorrow and the Desert of Loneliness are my companions, not a shelter of despair. They're my loyal companions that will escort me for as long as it takes, so that I can haughtily resist the Wind of the Desert...I pity you, Woman. Back then, I had met a girl who had lost her way home. Now, after such a long time, I meet the same person in the same place. But now she's lost the way to her soul. So be it...No one and nothing will stop me from rising!!! From the bottom of my heart, I believe that my Dawn has already begun..."

The young woman took a step back.

"Don't rush, Woman. I haven't finished yet. You know, the Desert has taught me a lot...My soul, like pure metal in a foundry, has become red-hot and melted inside of it. During my wandering, it was forged with patience and forbearance. It became a sharp blade ready to throw itself into any battle. I feel it's my duty to complete what I started back then. I have to help you find the way to your soul. Maybe that's why we cross paths again. It's time for me to reveal something. None of you really belongs to this world. All of you have come here for different reasons. This world is an illusion. An illusion that acts as a purgatory. You can choose. You can select the path of your destiny. You were born free but, with the passage of time, you deny yourselves your own freedom. You subjugate yourselves, wearing fetters similar to the ones I threw off with determination. So, you prefer slavery? What kind of logic dictates this? Reason...Yet another prison you surrounded yourselves with. Can you really define logic? Can you pinpoint where imagination ends and dream begins? There are so many things waiting for you to discover them. When was the last time you listened out for the Wind's song? The rustle of the leaves? The gurgling sound of water? When was the last time you read the stars? All these are trying to speak to you. Can't you hear them? You should know that, before I met the Spirits, my best friend was a small primrose. Everything lies in front of you, as long as you dare take a step...A single step is enough for you to reach out your hand. But the very idea scares the wits out of you. Believe me, there's nothing more horrible than an infertile land, where Death is roaming. Of course, you even ignore the very notion of Death...You too are unable to discern that even the Desert itself, with its tests and trials, has its own Life. If you see what I mean, then your heart will be broken. Don't forget that I was the one who passed judgement on humans. I was the one who discerned that they can do something better. Your attempt to prevent me from approaching them, especially right now, after all this, surely has ulterior motives!!! Go now, Woman. It's up to you if your words act as grafting in your own soul, or as poison, like you characterised my thoughts…"

25

The young woman was still silent and still. Her words, though, kept ringing in my ears. They came rushing in again and again to complete their task. Their aim was to take revenge on me for believing in my Wandering...

How could I fall prey to an illusion, though?

How could her Call be the trap of my illusion? Is it possible that she does not exist, since everything inside of me is overwhelmed with her? I saw her!!! I almost touched her!!!

Could I ever betray the omens and signs that have guided me so far? These too have been as patient and faithful companions as the Abyss of my Sorrow and the Desert of my Loneliness. Loyal patient and real, determined to carry on with me to the bitter End.

This night is so weird...

O Lady of Oblivion!!! Only for tonight, go back to the palaces of Shadows...

You, Shadows, stop whispering only for tonight...

I've never asked you for anything. Do me this favour only for

this strange night...

Take the tears of my agony for Redemption,

turn them into precious stones and keep them as a reward.

O Lady of Despair, I want to listen out for her Call!!!

I want her to come from afar like the melody of a Nightingale.

The Nightingale chooses the nights for its song.

It does so to entrance the Shadows.

They listen to it, engrossed in its beauty,
and forget to haunt the souls, until dawn breaks...
I'd give my all to see a ray heave into view like a thread
to take me out of my dark Labyrinth...
To lead me to a peak made of my aspirations!!!
To touch Infinity...
I want to see it waiting for me on that top!!!
Playing with the Stars as they dance around her...
Who could tell
if the Shine enveloping her is her own or that of the Stars?
Everone's dreams lie in each star...
Her name is written on my own star.
I'll do all I can to touch this Star!!!
No Sky can keep away from it forever...
How weird this night is...
Thoughts, be strong and crystal clear. Don't you ever betray or abandon me.
Not now that I need you so much!!!
Only you can allay the pain of her absence that is more acute
inside of me than ever!!!
This night is really strange...
A night misunderstood like the song of Loneliness...
It was night
when I saw your face painted on the Full Moon...
When I heard your call, like the one of the River God
inviting the souls to travel to Orion!!!
I want to reach the end of the world,there in the frozen fjords...
Where the colours travel with the Sky!!!
I want to see the Underworld,
snow-white sprawling beneath me,
humming a tune of Allure!!!
If only I had my wings back...
I want to go beyond my limits, flying...
Disappear, my Valkyrie!!!
It was night when you banished my nightmares!!!

The blade of my sword, drenched in my tears,
shimmers in the silver Moonlight!!!
The Elysian Fields would be an unbearable Inferno without you by my side...
My soul is yours!!!
Don't you ever dispute a Warrior's Word of Honour!!!
Everyone's afraid of the Night, yet I know...
Become my Moon to shine on the road of the Night!!!
Become my Dawn...
The dark of the Night is thicker before Dawn...
Night, I will give you my Sacred Oaths...
O misunderstood Night!!!
Like the Song of Loneliness...

With every passing day, her call is becoming stronger and stronger. Her presence and absence turned into two forces that alternately clash inside of me. My heart is a field carved by their traces...

My soul is forged out of patience and prudence. When will I put my weapons down and turn them into rays?

When will I bid farewell to the Desert of my Sorrow and the Abyss of my Loneliness?

When will I say good-bye to the icy-cold Wind of the Desert, while expressing my gratitude for what it taught me during my wandering?

O my beloved Thoughts, it's time you transformed and got the colour and wings that suit you. Come out of your cocoon. Turn into Moments...

Time, enigmatic Lord, you whose mantle surrounds everything...What charm must someone use to turn you into their precious ally?

How could someone trap your Oceans in a single drop? I want to trap this Drop!!! I want to add to it my Dawn and East, my expectations and dreams. I want to turn it into an amulet to put in my bosom.

The time has come, like a rushing river that won't come back. I'll never forget the Night, but I won't miss it either...

O Light! I'm ready to receive your embrace as I leave everything behind me...

The woman suddenly turned towards me. She looked different. She radiated!!!

She looked even more beautiful to me. I gaped at her for quite some time…

"My kind Aiaibamon," she said smilingly, "I've been listening to you all this time and your words light up my heart like a rainbow with colours of joy, hope and gratification. You really mean it when you say you didn't get to know me? I'm your Thoughts!!! You asked me to turn into Moments. Here I am before you with my human face. I was born inside of you the moment you opened your eyes to this world. I was a little girl when you reached the Source of the Spirits for the first time. I became a Woman when you went back to it. What you were taught made me who I am. Now I gave to go again. I have to complete the mission you assigned me. I must travel until I reach my destination. Until then, I will rest in humans' hearts sometimes and leave on them my signs like colours…"

While she was talking, I looked on in surprise. I couldn't believe what was going on.

I felt relieved amidst that craze, a sense of exultation in my perturbed spirit. At the same time, a strange Force pierced through my body.

I ran to her. I wanted to hug her once again, like I did at this very spot when she was still a little girl. But I didn't make it. As soon as I spread my arms open, she was gone…

I raised my eyes to the sky and cried out with renewed strength:

"O my beloved Thoughts!!! What can I say about your Faith and Devotion to me throughout my wandering? You turned into Moments when I asked you to. Of course, I couldn't reproach you just because I'm still trying to cherish that specific Moment, which will redeem me…Of course not! After all, I remained warrior even when my weapons were rusty and the wounds the battles inflicted on my body were countless. O my beloved Thoughts, you indulged me by becoming Moments!!! It's time for me to reflect if Time can grant me a wish…I'd like to hold you in one hand and in the other what I dreamt of, dream of and will dream of. Until I turn into a new dream myself!!! Maybe this way, you lead me to Maira, my own dream, which was made for me. Carry on with your journey. I feel pity for you, my personal Demons. My personal Demos, I pity you!!! I have no intention of fighting you. You didn't defeat me; I simply grew bored with you. The same fight over and over again. The only thing that differs is that you change your mask. You take on the form of either cunning Nomads of the Desert or unctuous reptiles. I see you arrayed opposite me fighting me, and I laugh. Yes, I laugh!!!

Your inarticulate cries ring in my head. They can no longer deaden the scream of my grandiosity. Your arrows are no longer capable of hitting my wings. Your poison is not enough to contaminate my blood. You have nothing new to offer me. You're no longer worthy enemies. I need worthy and befitting foes…It's time to overcome the Light and the Dark, to shake off the burden of the Fall. Just like my friend the little primrose did a while ago. But I will do it my way…It's time to open the eyes of my soul wide. To see clearly the things that were before me for so long. Now I'm ready to see them clearly. I am Aiaibamon of the Spirits, the Pyr-Kaa of humans!!! I am the Flame that came out of nowhere…My wandering is not futile. In fact, it starts just now. I will keep my wandering as a reward. It's time to part from the Desert of my Sorrow and the Abyss of my Loneliness. My East is close; now I can feel it, just like I can feel my transformation. Now I can understand that, with every passing moment, I take on my former looks. I will soon have my wings back. With my own wings, I will come to find you. This is the new oath I take…So much has changed since I sent you my thoughts for the first time; I am no longer alone. My relationships with humans are renewed. I can strike a balance between the two worlds. Humans felt my change. I am no longer repugnant to them. My Thoughts have been flying so far. Every now and then, they nestled in hearts to rest. Until they carried on with their journey to find you. From now on, my Thoughts will take shape to etch themselves in humans' hearts. My Wandering will be my legacy to humans.

26

"You're here," the familiar voice suddenly interrupted me.

I turned my gaze. I saw Kron-Ammoth. He wasn't alone. On his hand was perched a white dove. I recognised it. It was the dove I had released from the Cave of the Ancient Ones.

I gave them a puzzled look.

"What are you doing here together?" I asked.

The old man smiled. "It's time for me to complete the second story," he said.

"I don't get it," I stammered.

"You will," the old man continued. "It's time for you to learn everything. Listen to me carefully."

I shot him a perplexed glance.

"One of the worlds made by the gods was Sir-e-Lan. It's one of the first and most beautiful worlds inhabited by creatures made out of their ornaments. This world was ornamented by the green of nature, colourful flowers, three Suns that shone to show that it is a world made mainly out of Light and Fire as well as seven Moons that at nights shone on the gods' gifts — their colour a bright blue."

Upon hearing these words, I felt everything inside of me shake.

"So, this world exists, eh?" I let out a cry of despair.

"Yes, my dear friend, it exists," he answered. "The Gods adore this world of Sir-e-Lan. They always rejoice in seeing it from above. Erafel lived in Sir-e-Lan. He was a creature made of Light. Such was his joy and gratitude for the gods and their gifts that it overflowed inside Erafel. In order to show it to them, he greeted the three Suns every morning. In return, they gave him strength as he wandered around all day marvelling at the gods' creation. One day, as Erafel wandered around, he heard a song that came out of the forest. Never before had he heard anything like that. It was so majestic that he decided to go closer and check where it came from. He followed the song. When he neared it, he stopped short. He hid behind a rock until he saw the most beautiful thing he had ever laid his eyes on. Maira…"

When I heard her name, I felt all my senses on the alert. I jumped up. Kron-Ammoth smiled. He nodded to me to let him continue…

"Maira was a creature made of Fire. She liked wandering among the trees, admiring the flowers, even talking or singing to them. Erafel watched her lying among the flowers, singing and moving her hands, as if she were nodding to them. He felt his heart racing in a different way. It was like a part of her flame had begun to sear him within. He decided to approach her without hesitation. As soon as she sensed his presence, she withdrew at first. When she took a closer look at him, though, she felt his light radiate through her own heart. They fell head over heels in love. From that point onwards, Erafel and Maria were inseparable. They wandered happily around Sir-e-Lan, living their love affair with ineffable joy. Their love was so strong and beautiful that during the day the three Suns sent their smile, lending Maira's form a fiery beauty. The flowers filled with more colours. They gave off even more fragrant scents, while at night the seven Moons adorned with their light Erafel's blue winged form. The sky sent shooting stars like gold dust, as if sprinkled by a divine hand. Then, they turned into fireflies that danced around them…"

"Who's Maira? I see her image and it's so familiar to me!!! I feel her inside of me!!! Her presence surrounds me! She does exist, after all! Isn' she my call? Tell me, isn't she?" I screamed with all my might.

"Listen what happened next," the old man said with understanding.

I made quite an effort to keep in check the earthquakes that I began to unleash.

"Their days would pass amid this unprecedented joy. They gave place to the nights in an everlasting cycle. Still, they ignored the big danger lurking…In Sir-e-Lan lived Zeon-Moz, a powerful lord of darkness. When the gods made Sir-e-Lan, Zeon-Moz, who lorded it over all the creatures of darkness, was forced to flee to the bowels of the earth. Just like all the dark creatures, he hated the gods and God Creator as, because of their work, they had lost power in this world. Zeon-Moz led troops of dark creatures as well as those in the Underworld. Many of them, he used as spies, so that he would know what was happening on the surface at any time. From the moment the Fire and Light were created, Darkness will envy them till the end of Time. When Zeon-Moz was informed about Erafel and Maira's love affair, his hatred grew. He swore to destroy them. His jealousy and envy made him chafe at the union between Light and Fire. Time went by. Zeon-Moz couldn't find closure. He had to complete his plan. By destroying Erafel and Maira, he would take revenge on the gods and God Creator. He knew that the gods kept tabs on Sir-e-Lan. It was one of their favourite worlds. He feared that, if he attacked in front of their eyes, he would force the gods to intervene. He had to wait for the right time… Seasons came and went in an endless succession. Instead of abating, Zeon-Moz's hate grew stronger and stronger, and one day he received two important messages. In the first one, Ophis the Ancient, Zeon-Moz's friend and ally, informed him that the gods were busy making the last worlds out of the material that was left and all their attention was focused there. In the second, his allies told him that Erafel and Maira were in a forest. It was time for their seed of love to come into the world. Zeon-Moz's envy flared up even more. The news that the love and union of Light and Fire would bring a baby into the world addled his mind. He couldn't come to grips with the idea that this union would bear fruit. With the gods busy and Erafel and Maira, who were waiting for their baby, more vulnerable than ever before, Zeon-Moz thought this was the right time to attack them. He gathered his troop and drew up plans to attack. Ophis the Ancient advised him to use the 'Dark Breath', a spell that would darken the sky and prevent the three Suns of Sir-e-Lan to give strength to Erafel. Some of his trusted men, a select group with Zeon-Moz at the helm, advised him to attack Erafel as a decoy. The main troop would head for the mother and the baby to wipe them out. This was decided in the end. Zeon-Moz's troop set off. Following his spies' directions, they made for the forest, where Erafel and Maira were. In their path, all the creatures of Sir-e-Lan ran away to hide. There was dead silence all around. Erafel and Maira were under a tree, their baby about to come into the world. They were blissful and couldn't suspect the evil that was closing in on them. Zeon-Moz's troop reached the forest. He himself raised his stick and pronounced the words of the 'Dark Breath'. An otherworldly sound spread all over the place. The sky turned into a moonless night. Erafel and Maira looked around in puzzlement. They tried to understand what was going on. It was the time their baby had come into this world. Its voice was heard for the first time.

Erafel held his loved one and the baby in his arms. He kissed them tenderly, telling Maira not to leave that spot for any reason. He would go check the place around the forest. The forest was already surrounded by Zeon-Moz's hordes. When Erafel came out of the trees, he was attacked by his chosen ones. The rest of the troop moved towards Maira, as was planned."

I heard the old man, dumbfounded.

"Zeon-Moz and his chosen ones surrounded Erafel. The remaining troop reached the spot where Maira and the newborn baby were. With a cry, Erafel warned Maira to protect the baby in every way that she could. As a creature of Fire, she took out of her hands, which she reached out like an embrace, a fiery ring that grew bigger and bigger. In the end, this turned into a huge circle of fire that surrounded her and the newborn baby, protecting them both. Those dark creatures that happened to be caught up in the flames turned to ashes on the spot. As they burnt, their howls resounded throughout the place. The rest of the troop couldn't go any near them. Maira and the baby, safe now, were waiting for the outcome of the battle between Erafel and Zeon-Moz. The earth shook under the dark sky of Sir-e-Lan. Thunderbolts and lightning rent the air. All the creatures of Sir-e-Lan listened out silent and fearful, waiting for the outcome of that fierce battle. Even though Erafel couldn't get strength from the three Suns, he carried within the power of real Love, the feeling that his family was safe and well protected. He knew that the outcome of this battle would judge more things. One by one, Zeon-Moz's chosen men succumbed to Erafel's blows, until the two of them, the two almighty creatures, were left on the battlefield. At some point, Zeon-Moz seemed to have an advantage. He tried to pierce through Erafel's body with his blade at the base of his cane. But Erafel, with a swift move, parried his blow and lashed back. He ended up only with a small wound in his back."

Upon hearing all this, I felt an unbearable pain in my back again. The spear piercing right through me again and again. I put my fingers where I felt I used to have wings. I let out a cry of pain. The old man continued:

"Erafel's blow to Zeon-Moz was fierce. It wasn't enough to wipe him out, but it made him panic. Zeon-Moz realised that he had lost the battle. His troop beat a hasty retreat. The 'Dark Breath' dissipated across the sky of Sir-e-Lan. The Three Suns shone again. All the creatures got out of their hideouts to celebrate Erafel's victory. But their joy was short-lived. The revelry was cut short by Maira's cry of despair as she saw Erafel lying on the ground. She ran to him, holding his weak body. Erafel's body had lost almost all its shine. His eyes had turned pitch black. He could barely utter a word. All the creatures of Sir-e-Lan gathered around him. That was the first time it had ever rained in their place. Everyone looked at the raindrops in puzzlement. The creatures of Sir-e-Lan didn't know what sorrow or sadness meant. They didn't know what tears are. That was why the sky decided to shed some tears for their sake in the form of raindrops. At some point, where Erafel lay, appeared an old friendly face. He too was an almighty Wizard-Warrior. He had the ability to change forms and travel across the worlds. No one really knew who he was or where he came from. He had many friends in all the worlds, thanks to his travels. He narrated stories to the creatures of Sir-e-Lan every time he visited them. When he heard about the incident, thanks to his great experience as a Wizard, he figured out what had happened. The blade in Zeon-Moz's sceptre wounded Erafel while the 'Dark Breath' was still strong. This meant that Erafel was under its dark spell. He was very sad not to have made it earlier and taken part in the battle. He was even sadder as no one, not even himself, knew of an antidote to the specific spell. However, he knew what effects the spell would have on Erafel. With the passage of time, darkness would spread inside of him until it seized him completely. His consciousness and memory would be gone forever. That was very risky. Erafel was an almighty creature. Losing his memory and consciousness, he would easily be under Zeon-Moz's spell, with unpredictable consequences. Erafel's power should never be uncontrolled by himself, nor susceptible to someone like Zeon-Moz. He would soon have to come up with a solution, otherwise Erafel would have to be wiped out. Then, he remembered one of the last worlds made by the gods that he had recently visited: Gaia-Chthon. He thought of taking Erafel to Gaia-Chthon. Since he could change forms, he would give him a human body until he found another way to break the spell of the 'Dark Breath'. While Erafel had a human body, he would be harmless. He would be with him, discreetly watching him, for as long as they stayed in Gaia-Chthon, among humans. He also pointed out that Zeon-Moz had better not know anything about his plan, for as long as they were in Gaia-Chthon, Maira let out cries of despair. She couldn't leave or part from Erafel. Still, he listened to his friend's words. With as much strength as he had left, he whispered that Kron-Ammoth's thought was the best for the time being. With a heavy heart, she had no option but to agree.

She held her baby and placed it on Erafel, who smiled as he saw his wife and baby. The three of them said goodbye, locked in what might be their last embrace. They didn't know if they would ever see one another. After a while, his old friend the Wizard approached Erafel. It was his turn to hold him in his hands. After looking at everyone with a smile, which meant to impart a note of optimism, he mouthed some incomprehensible words. Shortly afterwards, he made a signal with his hand. Suddenly, they both disappeared before everyone's surprised eyes."

"Are you that friend?" I asked, wearied by pain. All these revelations washed away everything in me.

The old man didn't reply.

"Sir-e-Lan's creatures felt even sadder about Erafel's absence. The tears coming down from the sky in the form of raindrops got even thicker."

Precipitation spread all over my own firmament. It took on the form of tears in my eyes. I fell down on my knees and wept for a while. But the old man continued:

"When Erafel opened his eyes, he realised he was in the world of humans. He didn't remember who he was or where he came from. He knew nothing about his past. Inside of him was a faint recollection of a female figure. He wasn't sure, though, if that memory was real or simply a figment of his imagination. He faced many difficulties in the world of humans, seeking answers. Erafel couldn't remember his real name. Humans called him Pyr-Kaa, which in their ancient language meant 'the flame that came from nowhere'. The spirits called him Aiaibamon, which non their language means 'he who wanders all the time'. During his wandering, he made lots of friends. He met humans and various creatures, some of them belonging to the magic world. At some point, he obtained a sword made by a divine hand that became the extension of himself. All this time, he wandered around Gaia-Chthon, searching for answers. Many a time, he faced his own thoughts and feelings, desperate to know who he really is. Now everything's over. You know it all. You learnt who you are," said the old man, closing his eyes. He continued smilingly, his gaze fixed on me. "Without realising it, I was always with you during your wandering. Now it's time for you to become Light again and unite with the Fire forever!!!"

"And I kept my promise," said the white dove. "I told you I always keep my promises." It stopped short for a while, flapping its wings in front of me. Then, it disappeared once again, flying to the sky...

27

AFTERWORD

...One day, a White Dove appeared to Kron-Ammoth. It told him it was time to return the favour to Erafel. He had set it free long ago. That's why it would reveal to him the way in which to break the spell. It had promised him, after all.

The White Dove explained to Kron-Ammoth that the solution lay in the sword he had in his possession. This swore was alive with his own soul and made by a divine hand. It decided what blow to deal.

It could only wound without killing if it saw fit. It was present when Erafel held that sword in his hands.

The White Dove said that Erafel knew the 'Real Name' of the sword. As he knew it, Erafel could unleash all its powers, which meant it was time to break the spell.

Kron-Ammoth, as he was an experienced and powerful wizard, was well aware what 'Real Name' meant. Real Name was something sacred. It was what give each soul substance, making it unique. Thanks to this name, gods know everything.

By knowing the Real Name, one can not only fully unleash the powers of a soul, but also trap it, making it obey one.

Kron-Ammoth asked the White Dove how come it knew all this. It replied that the Queen of Snow had confided in it. It went to find her and keep its promise to Erafel. They made a deal. She revealed the secret, but Erafel was not supposed to know immediately.

He would have to visit her in her palace. She herself was seeking redemption through a deathblow. Only Erafel's sword would deal that blow.

The White Dove also pointed out that, since his soul had been enlarged, he could use this sword against himself. Other hands should hold it, pure and filled with genuine love.

Kron-Ammoth was elated. For the first time in his life, there was a solution and real hope to fulfil his purpose. His first thought was to go back to Sir-e-Lan and find Maira, so as to inform her about what he had learnt.

Maira never stopped thinking of Erafel. She often talked to him, as if he stood before her, his form in her thoughts, while she was longingly waiting for his return.

There was such a strong eternal bond between them that they always sensed each other's presence.

Upon hearing Kron-Ammoth's words, Maria was very hesitant at first, wondering about the consequences. What effect would such an action have on Erafel? She worried what might happen if they failed.

Kron-Ammoth convinced her that this was their only chance. He firmly believed that, even if they failed, the sword would never harm Erafel.

Maira was convinced. She agreed to use the sword. They deiced to go to Gaia-Chthon to find Erafel.

Erafel recognised Maira's form, that familiar face that he saw in his visions. His gaze was fixed on her. He was watching her, although he couldn't utter a word.

He wondered if the form he saw was real. After a long time, she was in front of him again. He wouldn't go near her, though. He feared that he might get burnt by the flames that surrounded her like full-size ornaments.

Maira was surprised to see Erafel. Her fiery figure was shining with desire to meet him. She knew the being trapped in that human body was her loved one. Yet, she hesitated to fall into his arms. She dreaded the idea of inflicting pain on his human body.

Erafel noticed that she was holding something in her arms that nestled in her bosom. When she realised that, she let her hands down.

A dazzling light gushed out of her arms. A baby's happy cry rent the air. He observed the eyes of this tiny creature for quite some time. It was smiling at him as it longingly moved its unformed wings and body.

Kron-Ammoth narrated to Erafel all the things the White Dove revealed to him. He explained that this was a once-in-a-lifetime opportunity to break the spell and for him to take on his real form after so long.

All this time he had been wandering around the world of humans may have seemed like an eternity to Erafel.

Time moves differently in every world...
There are times when Time
is a straight line like a golden thread,
while some others it becomes a circle.
A circle like two opposite rainbows
joined together,
where moments travel inside of it like colours.
That's where the end meets the beginning and vice versa.
Some other times, Time moves like fast-flowing water,
carrying and washing away
countless moments like drops.
Some other times yet, it becomes like a drop
that can include the waters of all the worlds
incessantly...

A broad smile etched across Erafel's lips upon hearing his old friend's words.

His eyes flicked between Kron-Ammoth and Maira. His heart was pounding every time they locked gaze.

He felt ready and eager to take any risk. This was a one-way street. Either nonexistence or return to where he really belonged. It was crunch time...

He willingly and impatiently lay on the ground just as Maira grabbed the LightBringer in her trembling hands. It didn't seem to bother or chafe at the unfamiliar hands that held it.

Erafel heaved a sigh.

It was a breath that released and turned away all his wounds as well as the darkness that accompanied him during his stay in the humans' world.

At first, Maira held the sword hesitantly.

While she held it, innumerable images of Erafel's wandering around humans' world flashed through her mind, making her hands tremble even more.

Seeing these pictures, she felt all Erafel's emotions, while he was inside the human body. At some point, her knees buckled. Letting out a cry of pain, she stuck the blade into his weak human body.

After a while, her hands still trembling, she clasped Erafel's soulless body.

Moments went by with no response. It seemed that life had oozed away from Erafel's body...

Maira was desperately calling out his name. She felt her eyes burn more than ever before.

At some point, drops of lava dripped down from her eyes onto Erafel's body. Little did she know she was shedding her own tears. The fact that she was in Gaia-Chthon had begun to rub off on her.

Fiery drops were pelting down like rain over his lifeless body. They were searing it. Then, they began to mingle with his blood. They trickled over the wound inflicted by the LightBringer as it was still stuck in his body.

As her fiery tears ran over Erafel's wound, a blue shine enveloped her. That very moment, their baby radiated more than ever before. The blue shine spread all over Erafel's body.

Suddenly, a blue winged form emerged from the soulless and motionless human body, which lay on the ground. Erafel woke up — he was his former self. He could remember everything.

He longingly clapped his wings to hold his fiery lover in his arms as well as the seed of their love. This flutter of wings ended in an eternal kiss, a perennial embrace.

They left the ground before the surprised eyes of the humans, who saw from afar a riot of colours across the sky. It was the moment the Light mingled once again with its eternal love, the Fire.

Many a time at nights around the fire, the elders narrated the story of Erafel. They spoke of his brave soul and his unwavering devotion to Maira. It was a message Gaia-Chthon was in need of...

Humans, more than ever before, need to feel beauty, emotions, hope and colour in their life and soul.

This is the story of Erafel. For those who already know or have just learnt how the Light *once fell in love with the Fire...*

THE END

www.ingramcontent.com/pod-product-compliance
Lightning Source LLC
LaVergne TN
LVHW020338200726
843507LV00012B/2410